SUGAR CREEK GANG
THE
WINTER RESCUE

Original title:
Further Adventures of the Sugar Creek Gang

Paul Hutchens

Adam

Tom Lanning

MOODY PRESS

ISBN 0-8024-4803-8

Moody Press, a ministry of the Moody Bible Institute, is designed for education, evangelization and edification. If we may assist you in knowing more about Christ and the Christian life, please write us without obligation to: Moody Press, c/o MLM, Chicago, Illinois 60610.

27 29 30 28 26

Printed in the United States of America

1

BEGINNING TO WRITE a story is something like diving under a cold shower or taking the first plunge into Sugar Creek when the water's cold. It's hard to get started. But after I'm in, paragraph deep, and my thoughts are splashing around a little, it certainly feels grand. My words go swimming and diving and having a good time— in ink of course, 'cause I always use a fountain pen when I write. Hurrah! Here I am already started, trudgeoning along faster than anything on a brand new Sugar Creek Gang story. Say! Does it ever feel good to be writing again!

In just a minute I'll explain what I mean by "trudgeon," that is I'll explain it when I'm telling you about the last time our gang went in swimming before school started that fall.

That was kind of a sad day for us—that last Saturday. Especially for Little Jim, but I'll have to tell you about it even though I don't like to write about sad things.

Say, I wonder how many miles the point of a boy's fountain pen travels while he's writing a story, a big long story like this one's going to be. Hundreds and hundreds of miles, I guess, although I never figured it up. Not liking arithmetic very well is the main reason. Ho hum!

None of us boys wanted school to begin that fall even though we knew every boy ought to have an education if he wanted to amount to anything.

Well, at last that wonderful summer was over and we knew there wasn't any way to get out of going to school. Going to school is like starting in swimming too. After you get in, it's all right and it's good for you. It washes all the ignorance off a boy and makes him feel good.

Well, it was Saturday, the last Saturday of our summer and it was noon at our house. I took the last bite of my three-cornered piece of blackberry pie, chewed it as long as I could because it tasted so good I hated to swallow it, then looked across the table at my dad's big bushy blackish-red eyebrows to see if he was going to say no when I asked him if I could go swimming that afternoon.

Charlotte Ann, my little three-months-old, black-haired baby sister, was in her little rubber-wheeled, blue and white bassinet, kinda half lying down and half sitting up like a baby bird in a nest full of pillows. She was smiling like she was happier than anything, and was gurgling and drooling, which means she was making little

4

bubbles of saliva tumble out of her soft little lips. And her arms and legs were going like four windmills whirling all at once. Her pretty little ears looked like the halves of little dried peaches which somebody had glued onto the side of her head.

She's getting prettier all the time, I thought, *if only she doesn't get red hair like mine*. I could see that someday maybe there'd be freckles on her little nose, and I felt sorry for her 'cause I had freckles myself and didn't like them. In fact, there were freckles all over my face.

Dad's big eyebrows were kinda halfway between up and down, and Mom was busy eating her pie and smiling back at Charlotte Ann. In fact, Dad was looking at Charlotte Ann too, as if Bill Collins—that's my name—wasn't even important any more. I had had to take second place at our house ever since Charlotte Ann was born. That's what a boy has to do when a new baby comes to his house to live.

I sighed, thinking about how hot it was and looking over the top of a stack of soiled dishes in the sink by the window. I was wishing I was out of doors running through the woods toward the spring where I knew Dragonfly, Poetry, Circus, Big Jim, and Little Jim would be waiting for me and where old Sugar Creek would be almost screaming for us to come and jump in. He wanted to prove to us his water was still warm enough to swim in, even if it was going to be fall pretty soon and then winter and he'd have to have a cold sad face until the spring rains came and washed it again and the sun melted his ice coat and made him happy. Say, if I was old Sugar Creek, about the only time I could ever by happy would be when a gang of boys was swimming in my warm, sparkling water.

Well, I looked away from the window without seeing the dishes and was looking at the little scotch terrier design on Charlotte Ann's bassinet when I said, "Look at her wave her arms and legs, Dad! I'll bet she could swim without even having to learn how."

Say, my dad could read my thoughts just like I could read an electric sign on a city store. You should have seen his big eyebrows drop kinda like a grassy ledge caving in along Sugar Creek. "Those aren't swimming movements," he said, taking a last bite of pie. "Those are the movements a boy's hands make when he is drying the dishes." That's why I was the last one of our gang to get to the spring that day.

It seemed like it took almost an hour to wipe those dishes. While I was doing them, I looked down at Charlotte Ann who was still making spit bubbles with her lips, which were kinda like two red rose petals all wet with dew, and I thought, *Go on, little innocent child, and have your play! Someday you'll grow up—if you ever do!—and then you'll have to work!"* And for a minute I was mad at her for not growing faster.

Pretty soon the dishes were all done and set away and I was feeling happy again. I made a dive for my straw hat which was on the floor in a corner where I wasn't supposed to put it. Mom always wanted me to hang it up. A jiffy later I was outdoors, my bare feet carrying me lickety-sizzle down the path through the woods to the spring.

I tell you, it was great to be with the gang again. Maybe I'd better tell you about our gang just in case you may not have read my other Sugar Creek Gang stories—although it seems like everybody in the world ought to know about us, with all the newspaper publicity we got after Little Jim killed the fierce old mother bear. If he hadn't, that old bear might have ripped him all to pieces with her horrible teeth and claws or maybe hugged him to death like bears do.

Well, this was our gang: Big Jim, our leader, who was so big he had actually shaved his fuzzy mustache once and who had been a boy scout; Little Jim, a grand little guy with blue eyes like Charlotte Ann's and the best Christian in the world; Circus, our acrobat who, right that very minute, was sitting on the first limb of a maple sapling looking like a chimpanzee; Poetry, who was short and globular—which means "round, like a globe,"—and who knew a hundred and one

7

poems by heart; Dragonfly, whose eyes were very large like a dragonfly's eyes are. He could see better than the rest of us.

The new member of our gang was there, Little Jim's pet bear, the little black baby bear whose savage old mother got killed in my last story. That little brown-nosed baby bear was the cutest, most awkward little fellow you ever saw. He could already do half a dozen tricks. We had named him Triangle because there was a little three-cornered white spot on his chest like black baby bears sometimes have. Little Jim had a new leather collar on Triangle's neck with the word *Triangle* engraved on it. And Little Jim's favorite Bible verse was right below that: "Train up a child in the way he should go, and when he is old he will not depart from it."

Say! I never saw anybody in my life who was a better Christian than Little Jim, and he wasn't ashamed of being one either. In fact, he was proud of it.

Poetry had made up a good poem about Triangle which started like this:

> Black little, bad little, brown-nosed bear,
> Frowzy little fellow with a tail that isn't there.

You know, bears don't have tails except for a stubby little stump that looks kinda like a dog's tail that has been cut off. Only Triangle's tail didn't stand straight up like a tail does on a happy dog, but it hung down kinda like a sheep's tail does.

As I told you before, we wouldn't allow any girls to belong to our gang because none of us boys liked girls very well. Girls are such funny things, always scared of mice and screaming whenever they see a spider or something. Circus *did* have a kinda nice ordinary sister whom I'd made up my mind I was going to kill a spider for as soon as I got a chance, which I didn't get until school started that fall.

Well, we wouldn't let any girl belong to our gang but we did decide to let Little Jim's bear belong. Bears aren't afraid of mice. They even eat them. Triangle liked mice, frogs, fish, ants, bees and their honey, blackberry pie, and things like that. We couldn't let him eat too much honey or sweet things at one time or he'd have gotten sick.

Say, you should have seen that little fellow swim! He was as playful as a kitten in the water. And he was only about three times as big as a big tomcat, although he was growing very fast.

Well, there we all were, all of us barefoot, knowing that next Monday we'd have to wear shoes all day at school, and feeling sad because of it. All of a sudden, Circus—who, as I told you, was sitting on the first limb of a maple sapling—let out an Indian war whoop, slid down

9

the tree, and started running toward the swimming hole, yelling back over his shoulder, "Last one in's a bear's tail!" In less than a jiffy all the gang was running right after him as fast as they could go—all except Little Jim and Triangle and me. That mischievous little rascal of a bear had evidently made up his mind he didn't want to go in swimming, 'cause he wouldn't even get up when Little Jim told him to. He just lay there in the sun like he was too lazy or sleepy to move.

I caught hold of the chain which was fastened to Triangle's collar, and both of us pulled and scolded until Triangle growled a disgusted sort of growl and whined lazily. That made Little Jim decide to give him a switching with a little willow switch, which is what you have to do with baby bears when they won't obey you.

That switching helped a little, like a good licking does a boy for awhile, and pretty soon we were on our way to the swimming hole. I noticed when we were kinda half pulling Little Bear along behind us that the collar around his neck was a little bit too loose and maybe we'd better tighten it another notch. But Little Jim said he thought that'd be too tight and might choke Triangle. Besides, the collar was locked on and the key was at Little Jim's house almost a quarter of a mile away.

Pretty soon we were at the swimming hole.

Because Triangle was still stubborn and didn't want to go in the water and was cross when we threw him in and wouldn't do any of his tricks for us, Little Jim decided to tie him to an ash sapling up on the shore. "Smarty," Little Jim said. "I'm going to tie you up behind this big stump so you can't even watch us. That's your punishment for not cooperating," which is a word our teacher uses on our report cards at school. When we don't obey her or join in with the others in their play or work, she gives us a check mark in the square which says, "Does not cooperate." That fall there was only one of the Sugar Creek Gang which had a check mark there, but I won't tell you which one of us it was 'cause I don't think my parents would want anybody to know.

Each one of our gang had his favorite style of swimming. Little Jim used the breaststroke which made him look like a white, swimming frog in the water. Circus used the crawl stroke. In fact, most of us did. That's the kind of stroke many fast swimmers use. But Poetry, being an expert swimmer, had a newfangled stroke called the "trudgeon." He just lay face down in the water, rolled his barrel-like body from side to side, and swung his arms in long over-arm movements, each arm taking turns. His feet under the water worked like my mom's big silver-colored scissors do when they're cutting out a new dress for Charlotte Ann.

All the time I was in swimming I kept thinking about little brown-nosed Triangle up there on the shore behind the stump, which was behind a clump of willows, and I thought, what if the little fellow should slip the collar over his head and run away? Or what if somebody who wanted to steal him and sell him to the zoo should sneak up and slip the collar off his neck and carry him away, the little fellow not having any mother to take care of him. And pretty soon it'd be fall and then winter. There was a big cornfield right there by the willow too, and a baby bear might get lost in a cornfield.

It was more than an hour later when we sort of came to ourselves and realized we'd better get dressed and go home. The next day would be Sunday, and we'd have to polish our shoes and do some extra chores Saturday so we wouldn't have to do them Sunday. As I told you in my last book, all of our gang went to church and Sunday school on Sundays. We all felt sorry for any boy who didn't want to go and for all the kids whose parents didn't think a boy's soul was as important as the rest of him.

Imagine a boy going to school five days a week to learn reading, writing, arithmetic, geography, history, and other important things and not go to church just once a week to learn about the Bible which is the most important book in the world. It tells you how to be saved, which is more important than being educated.

Well, Dragonfly got dressed first and ran up the bank toward the old stump behind the willow to untie Triangle, with Little Jim and me right at his already-dirty bare heels, when all of a sudden Dragonfly stopped dead in his tracks and cried, "Hey! He's GONE! Triangle's GONE! Somebody's stolen him!"

2

WE COULDN'T BELIEVE OUR EYES, and yet we had to 'cause Triangle was gone and only the chain and the leather collar were there. Little Jim stood with the collar in his hand, looking down at the Bible verse on it with great big tears in his eyes. Pretty soon a couple of his tears splashed out and fell on my bare toes 'cause I was standing right close to him.

I gulped and got mad instead of crying because the leather collar had been cut in two with a knife. Somebody's boy hadn't been trained up in the way he ought to go. Whoever it was, I thought, it must have been somebody that didn't like us very well, that is, if he had just cut the collar so the bear could run away and hadn't stolen him.

Right away I thought of the Till boys who lived on the other side of Sugar Creek. Their father was an infidel, and they hadn't been to Sunday school and church in their lives. They belonged to a rough gang of boys which our gang had licked last summer in the Battle of

14

Bumblebee Hill, the new name we gave that hill after the fight.

We were all standing there and all talking at once with nobody listening to anybody when Dragonfly, who had been looking around a little, yelled, "Hey! Come here quick!"

In a half jiffy we all saw what he saw: bear tracks going down a corn row, right behind a man's shoe prints which were going in the same direction!

With Big Jim and Dragonfly in the lead, and with the rest of us following, Little Jim carrying Triangle's chain and cut collar, we felt kinda like a funeral procession, I guess. Only we knew we weren't on our way to any graveyard unless it was to the little bear's grave. I never realized how much I liked the mischievous little rascal until right that minute. Of course, the man, or whoever it was had stolen him, would sell him to a zoo and he'd get plenty to eat, but he'd have to live in a cage all the time, I thought.

We kept on hurrying through the cornfield, following Dragonfly and Big Jim who were following Triangle's tracks. We were especially careful not to let the sharp edges of the sword-shaped corn blades cut our eyes.

All of a sudden we came out on the other side of the field where there was a rail fence and a road. There the footprints disappeared, and we couldn't find them. That meant, if my thoughts were right, that the man who had taken him and led him away had probably climbed into a truck or car and driven away with him.

Well, we couldn't find any more tracks, so Big Jim went back to study the ones we'd been following, which was hard to do 'cause we'd all foolishly walked right along in them and most of them were covered up with bare feet tracks. Once Big Jim stooped down and looked a long time, then he called us and said, "These tracks are a lot older than the bear's tracks. There are little dust spatters in them!"

Well that settled that, and my idea was crazy, but just the same I hated to give up my swell idea. Of course, if I was wrong, it meant that Triangle had just run away and we'd probably find him, or our folks would, or somebody.

It wasn't far from where we were to the swamp and the old sycamore tree where so many important things had happened, so we went there to talk things over and to decide what to do. Big Jim called a meeting, and it was while we were sitting there in the grass with a lot of old gray-haired dandelions around us, looking like old men that didn't have much longer to live, that I got to thinking about Old Man Paddler who lived up in the hills. He had taught us boys so many important things and had showed Little Jim how to teach Triangle to dance a jig. Old Man Paddler had had a pet bear cub himself once when he was a little boy almost seventy-five years ago. Say, that little Triangle of a black little, bad little, brown-nosed bear had liked Old Man Paddler almost as well as he had Little Jim.

Old Man Paddler wore long white whiskers and was the kindest old man you ever saw, and he was happy. I heard my dad say once that the devil doesn't have any happy old men, which means that if you want to be happy when you're old, you'll have to start being a Christian when you're young.

That kind old man knew all about bears and pretty nearly everything else. You could ask him almost anything and he could answer you. My dad said he had been a lawyer once. He had had three children, all of them boys, but none of them had lived to be over twelve years of age. Then his wife had died too and left him all alone in the world, and he had been so sad that he had built a cabin up in the hills and lived alone. And after that he'd rather do something for boys than anything in the world, on account of him not having any.

Well, while we were sitting under the old sycamore tree talking about what had happened to Little Jim's bear, I kept on thinking about Old Man Paddler who had been a lawyer once and I thought we might ask him what to do about getting the bear back.

Dragonfly thought we ought to tell the police, so that in case he had been stolen instead of having run away, they'd put detectives on the case.

Poetry didn't like the idea at all because he said the Sugar Creek Gang were better detectives than any old policemen detectives, meaning he thought Poetry himself was pretty good.

"Didn't we catch the bank robber without any help?" Poetry asked, which was true.

"And didn't we find Old Man Paddler and save his life? And didn't we kill a bear all by ourselves?" Poetry finished.

Just when Circus rolled over and turned a somersault backward and said excitedly, "I'll go and get my dad's big hounds," meaning his dad's big, long-eared, long-tongued, sad-faced hunting dogs. "And if we let 'em smell Triangle's collar," Circus explained, almost yelling, "they'll follow his tracks with their noses and find where he went."

Well, that looked like the best thing to do, so we voted on it like grown-ups do in their business meetings. Poetry made what is called a "motion," saying, "I move we get Circus' hounds and let them trail Triangle."

Dragonfly said, "I second the motion," meaning "I'm in favor of that too."

Then Big Jim said in a very business-like voice, "It has been moved and seconded that we get

18

Circus' hounds and that we let them trail Triangle. Are you ready for the question?" That meant he wanted to know if we were ready for him to ask how many of us wanted Circus to get his dad's dogs.

So I piped up and said, "Question."

Big Jim cleared his throat and said, "All in favor of the motion raise your right hand."

In a jiffy all our kinda dirty right hands were up in the air except Little Jim's, and it wasn't on account of him not knowing how to vote either. I looked at his eyes because I saw him give his little head a toss like he always does when he wants to get tears out of his eyes without letting anybody know there were any there.

Then Big Jim said, "Those opposed use the same sign." And Little Jim's hand shot up like he was waving good-bye to somebody he liked very much and wouldn't ever see again.

"The motion is carried," Big Jim said, which meant that most of us wanted the dogs, and the meeting was over. Pretty soon we'd all run over to Circus' house to get his dad's hounds, and they'd put their noses on the collar and on Triangle's tracks, and sniff. Then they'd go bawling and howling on the trail, following the tracks with their noses which can smell fresh animal tracks better than a hungry boy can smell raw-fried potatoes at suppertime.

Little Jim was too brave to cry but his voice

sounded like it had tears in it when he said, stuttering a little, "Th-they'll c-catch T-Triangle and b-bite him and m-m-maybe t-t-t-tear him to pieces with their big sharp teeth!

So, without calling a meeting, we decided right away, for Little Jim's sake, not to get the hounds. Something had to be done, though, 'cause you can't let a baby bear run loose in a neighborhood; for he is bound to get into trouble. And maybe somebody who doesn't know he's a pet will see him and shoot him, or maybe somebody's dogs will kill him.

We finally decided to keep our eyes open and to go on home and tell our folks he was lost and have them keep their eyes open for him too. We all felt sorry for Little Jim as well as for ourselves, because we all liked that "frowzy little fellow with a tail that isn't there." When anything is lost, you like it even better. Say! Do you know what Little Jim said to me that afternoon when he left our house to go on home? He was always piping up and saying something important like that. He said, "I'll bet that's why Jesus likes boys so well, 'cause so many of them are lost. I'll bet he likes Tom Till an awful lot." And that made me remember I'd promised my Sunday school teacher I'd go over and see little red-haired Tom Till and try to get him to come to Sunday school tomorrow, and I hadn't done it yet.

As I said, the very minute I knew Triangle was lost, I thought of the Till boys but especially of their mean-faced, hook-nosed father who drank whiskey and whose words most of the time were as filthy as a mud puddle in a barnyard. I don't know why I thought of him but I did, and I felt sorry that Little Tom Till had to have that kind of a daddy. I was afraid of Big John Till too. The only time I wasn't afraid of him was that time he'd tried to give Circus' dad whiskey, and I had been so mad that I'd dived right into him red head first and started socking him on the nose and the chin and in the stomach with my fists. I got knocked flatter'n a waffle for doing it.

Well, a promise was a promise, so after supper I decided to go over to Tom Till's house and while I was there to look around a little to see if I could find a brown-nosed bear cub with a white triangle on his breast. I wondered what would happen if I did find him or what if John Till would get terribly mad at me for asking Tom to go to church with us tomorrow.

As soon as supper was over, I told Mom what I'd promised my teacher. Then I went in and looked at Charlotte Ann who was asleep in her little Scotty dog bassinet. I took a big breath of fresh air and tried to feel brave, and I said to sleeping Charlotte Ann, "Little sister, I'm going to war now. I may come back with a broken

21

arm or a black eye or something, but duty calls me."

I was thinking about Tom Till and hoping something very important about him, so I ran upstairs to get my New Testament. While I was in my room, I shut the door for a minute and went down *kersmack* on both of my knees, which is what I do when I pray. My dad says it takes a brave man to get down on his knees and pray all by himself, and I guess most people are too big a coward to do it.

Anyway my knees were just beginning to feel a little bit tired on the hard floor, when all of a sudden the door burst open and my dad came in.

"Oh, excuse me," Dad said. "I didn't know you were here. I thought you'd gone."

I looked up quick and there were tears under his big eyebrows. Then without even looking at me, he gave me a great big hug and said, still not looking at me, "I'd rather have a praying boy than any other kind, Bill. I'm sorry I interrupted you." Then he turned and went out and shut the door, and I finished what I was doing and went downstairs. When I got there my dad was in our front room standing beside Mom, looking down into Charlotte Ann's bassinet, and he and Mom were hugging each other, which I always liked to see them do. Then with my heart as light as a feather I went outdoors and jumped on my bicycle and pedaled down the road and across the Sugar Creek bridge toward Tom Till's house, wondering all the time if anything important was going to happen to me before I got back.

3

WHEN I WAS ABOUT halfway across the bridge, I stopped for a minute, stood my bicycle up against the railing on the east side, and looked at my long shadow which the sun made of me on the water, and I looked like a great big giant a hundred feet tall. I didn't feel like one, though, 'cause I remembered the sore jaw I'd had for nearly a week after John Till knocked me down that day under the elder bushes. Then I rode on across the bridge.

I always liked to hear the planks shaking when I went across. Some of the floorboards were loose and made a rattling noise whenever I rode over them. Sometimes, when I was at home in bed, I'd wake up in the middle of the night, hearing somebody's car or a horse and buggy going across.

The nearer I got to Tom Till's house the more queer I felt inside, and I think my heart must have been acting like Circus turning a lot of somersaults. The house that Tom Till lived in wasn't much of a house but that wasn't his fault.

Besides, it's the kind of people that live in a house that's important anyway. Tom and Little Jim had been friends ever since Little Jim had killed the ferocious old mother bear and maybe saved Tom's life. And even though Tom and I had given each other a black eye in that gang fight, we kinda liked each other anyway even though each one of us had red hair.

I stopped at their battered old gate, afraid to go in. I kept my eyes peeled for Triangle or John Till or Tom's big brother Bob, who was bigger even than Big Jim and almost as good a fighter.

Just that minute I glimpsed a bright red head of hair peeping around from behind a walnut tree and I knew it was Tom Till. He looked like he hadn't had a hair-cut all summer.

"Hello," I said, and Tom called back, "Hello."

"Want to play catch?" I asked, and took a big orange out of my pocket and threw it to him. I hadn't intended to throw it so high, but, say, that little fellow leaped up in the air and caught it with one hand, which meant he'd make a good player on our school ball team that fall.

Pretty soon we were lying down in the grass behind the fence, talking about different things. All the time I was wishing I'd tell him why I'd come over to his house, but I was afraid to. I could feel my New Testament in my pocket and I kept thinking about Little Jim's favorite verse which was in the Old Testament in Proverbs 22:6. But I was thinking especially of the story of the boy in the New Testament who gave his lunch to Jesus one day, and Jesus had fed a whole crowd of people with it. I wanted to tell Tom Till that Jesus liked boys and had actually died on the cross to save them, but — Well, I just couldn't for a minute.

Pretty soon though, I decided it was silly to be afraid, so I said, "I promised my Sunday school teacher I'd ask you to go to Sunday school with me tomorrow."

He had the orange all peeled and was dividing it in half with his dirty hands, the orange kinda washing off some of the dirt. Say! Do you know what? He handed me the cleanest half of the orange and said, "Maybe I *can* come. I'm going to get some new clothes in town tonight. Dad's made a lot of money this week and he's going to get me a new suit and shoes and everything."

I was so surprised 'cause I didn't know his dad had been working. For about nine seconds I couldn't do anything but stare at him 'cause I wondered where John Till had got all the money. I wiped off some of the dirt from my piece of orange and ate it and thought about Triangle and wondered if maybe he was already in a zoo somewhere or maybe riding along in an automobile.

Then I started telling Tom about the boy's lunch which was a couple of fish and five little buns, called loaves.

"Where'd the boy get the fish?" Tom wanted to know.

I'd never thought about that, so I said, "I don't know, but maybe he'd been fishing in Lake Galilee. They say fishing was awful good there. I'll bet the boys who lived close to the lake had a lot of fun fishing and swimming and things. I'll bet Jesus Himself went fishing when he was a boy."

"Was Jesus a boy once?" Tom asked, surprised.

"Sure," I said. "He was even a little baby once. But He was up in heaven first, where He'd been all the time and where He was when He made the world and all the stars and things. Then He came to our earth to be our Saviour, but the people didn't want to be saved, so they treated Him mean and even crucified Him and—"

"What's *crucified* mean?" Tom asked. Imagine him not knowing that! Well, I explained to him different things, like my dad and mom and my Sunday school teacher had explained them to me —and Little Jim, 'cause Little Jim could explain it in boy's language which made it easier to understand.

Then Tom Till said, "My daddy doesn't believe in Jesus."

Just that minute I heard loud talking in their

house, and it was Big Bob Till talking back to his mother and saying, "I won't do it! I *hate* wiping dishes! You *never* let me do anything I want to!"

Say! I felt my temper starting to catch on fire. Then I heard their back screen door open and slam shut, and I saw Big Bob Till shuffle out and grab his long cane fishing pole and start off toward the creek, but I couldn't see him very well. I was so angry 'cause I thought how his mother must feel, and do you know? I wanted to jump up and run after Big Bob Till and give him a terrible licking. I just wanted to sock him and sock him and sock him!

But I didn't. Instead I looked over at Little Tom and I said, without knowing I was going to, "Let's you and me go in and help your mother with the dishes," which we did.

I guess I never felt so polite in my life as I did right that minute, and especially while we were walking around in their kitchen, drying the dishes and setting them away. Every now and then, when Tom's kinda sad-faced mother wasn't looking, I'd look at her out of the corner of my eye, and do you know? She looked like just any ordinary mother who could be awful happy if she had a chance.

And the next day in church, when our new minister said it was sin that caused all the heart-aches in the world, I felt something inside of me just boiling up like a teakettle of water when it gets hot. I wanted to take a great big gospel sword and go running through the world and cut all the sin in all the world all to pieces.

I decided if Bill Collins or anybody that looked like him ever talked mean to his mother or wouldn't help her when she wanted him to and was too lazy to work, I'd sock him too. Lazy old Bill Collins! I tell you I was mad, even at myself!

Well, when we were through helping Tom's mom, I remembered I still had some chores to do at home, so I said, "Don't forget that Sunday school starts at ten. Be at our house at a quarter till and you can ride with us."

I climbed on my bicycle and pedaled for home as fast as I could.

4

AT A QUARTER TO TEN the next morning, Tom Till came over to our house in his new suit and shoes and with his hair cut, looking like an ordinary boy.

He sat right beside me in our Sunday school class, and I tell you it felt good to think I'd invited him to come.

It was a grand Sunday school lesson, all about a blind man getting his eyesight back again, and all that Jesus had to do was to reach out and touch his eyes. I thought how that in the battle of Bumblebee Hill Tom had blacked my eye and how I'd hated him so much I couldn't see straight. And now I didn't hate him anymore,. and I decided maybe Somebody'd touched my eyes and healed me.

Little Jim sat on the other side of Tom Till, and, in spite of myself, every time I looked down and saw Tom's new shoes with their shining black leather, my mind went splashing and diving along on the mystery of the lost bear.

After church was over, when I got a chance,

I told Little Jim why I thought maybe Tom Till's father had stolen Triangle. And do you know what Little Jim did? He kinda smiled with great big tears in his eyes and said, "I'm awful sorry to lose Triangle but I'd rather have Tom Till have a new suit and shoes and go to Sunday school than to have a pet bear." Then that brave little fellow gave his head a quick toss like he'd done yesterday and shook most of the tears out of his eyes. He dabbed the rest of them dry with his handkerchief and said, "Let's you and me have a secret." He made me promise I wouldn't tell anybody about what I thought I knew, and I kept my promise.

In fact, I'm glad I *didn't* tell anybody because that same day after dinner I found out that Triangle hadn't been stolen at all, although I knew it was a mean trick to cut the beautiful new collar and let the little cub loose. Whoever had done it, I thought, must have been somebody who didn't like the Sugar Creek Gang very well.

As soon as dinner was over at our house, Dad and I washed and dried the dishes, which we always do on Sunday because it's kinda like saying thank you to Mom for the especially nice dinner she cooked for us. Only it takes a lot longer to do the dishes than to just say two little words.

Charlotte Ann was supposed to be taking her nap and wasn't on account of being disgusted about something, so she was doing what all babies do when they feel that way. I didn't like to hear her cry so I went to our big swing and sat there waiting for Little Jim to come over to play with me. Dad took a walk down in our orchard, where he had his very best hive of bees with a whole lot of honey in it which he was going to sell before long and buy me a new suit.

Pretty soon I heard Dad calling, "Bill! Come here quick!" As soon as I could get out of the swing without jumping out, which is dangerous if you're swinging very high, I ran out into the orchard to where Dad was.

Dad was pointing to something under a big apple tree and he said with a big voice, "Look what your famous pet bear did to my very best beehive while we were in church this morning!"

Say! There was his biggest and best beehive turned over on its side with the upper part of it burst open and with maybe a thousand bees swarming in every direction, madder than anything.

I knew bears liked honey very very much, but Old Man Paddler had told us it wasn't good for them to eat too many sweets because bears are what is called "carnivorous" animals. That means their main food is flesh of some kind, and too much honey or syrup will make them sick, just like too many green apples or grapes would a boy.

I was standing looking at that turned-over

beehive, glad that Triangle was still alive but worrying a little as to what might happen to him if he got a stomachache, when Dad said, "Do you know how much honey there was in that upstairs part of the hive?"

I said, "No. How much?"

He said, "About twenty pounds! I know because I looked in yesterday. Your bear has eaten at least fifteen pounds of honey that I was going to sell to help pay for your suit, you know."

In my mind I could see Little Jim's frowsy, brown-nosed baby bear with his fat little sides bulging with maybe twenty pounds of honey, or even twenty-five, if he could eat that much, and with his nose all swollen where the bees had stung him, which bees do when you try to take their honey, and I felt very sorry for him. I knew he'd be sick and he might even die if somebody didn't find him and take care of him.

Well, my dad and our new minister and Little Jim's dad and Circus' dad and some of the musicians from our church were going to hold a gospel meeting in a big jail in the city that afternoon where there were a lot of men and older boys who hadn't been trained up in the way they ought to go. That's why Little Jim and his mom came over to our house that afternoon —to wait until the jail meeting was over.

Pretty soon Little Jim and I were out in our orchard looking at the overturned beehive, without getting close enough for the bees to see us and think we were the ones that had broken up their home. Bees aren't able to see very well, and sometimes I don't think they think at all.

Say, all of a sudden I got to thinking that what I wanted to do more than anything else right that minute was to find that little bear so we could nurse him back to health in case he was sick. I knew the quickest way to find him was to put Circus' dad's big dogs on his trail. I thought if Big Jim and Circus would hold the dogs back by a strong leash, we could follow right along behind them and find the bear, and the dogs wouldn't hurt him 'cause we wouldn't let them. Of course I knew I'd have to make Little Jim see how important it was first or he wouldn't let us do it.

I guess I was thinking about how much fun it would be too. In fact, I was. Well, I told Little Jim what my dad said had happened, and Little Jim looked at the broken beehive and said, "I wonder how much he ate." I said, "Maybe ten or fifteen or even twenty pounds."

Little Jim stooped down to tie his shoe string which had come untied. While he was still stooped over, he said with a grunt, "Do you suppose he got stung very bad?"

"Maybe a thousand times," I said. Then remembered that bees can't sting through a bear's heavy fur. They *can* sting his nose and mouth though, unless he puts his paws up to protect himself. Even then, when he's eating honey he's bound to get stung pretty bad.

"He probably ate a thousand bees too," I said, " 'cause the bees crawl all over the honey all the time, and he might get a terrible stomach-ache."

Then Little Jim said, "Do you suppose the bees could sting him on the inside?"

"They might," I said. "Anyway, he'll probably need a doctor." Then I reminded Little Jim of what Old Man Paddler had said about bears being carnivorous and how they shouldn't eat too much honey or syrup or they'd have what is called "dietary" trouble.

I guess that long word scared Little Jim 'cause the first three letters of it spell the word *die*. Anyway when I mentioned Circus' dad's hounds and explained how we could hold them from hurting that fat little round Triangle, Little Jim changed his mind, and in less than two minutes we were on my bicycle pedaling down the road toward Circus' house. He lived right across the road from Big Jim. Well, Poetry was already there, so that was all of us except Dragonfly who couldn't have been with us anyway because his parents had gone to another town to visit a cousin of his. The reason Circus' dad had gone to the jail meeting too was because he was going to give what is called a "testimony" so all the men and boys in the jail could believe that even a drunkard could be saved if he would repent of his sins and believe on the Lord Jesus Christ. Say! Circus' dad hated whiskey worse than his big sad-faced hounds hated a skunk.

Well, we took two of those big dogs, Big Jim holding the leash of one and Circus the other, and away we went by a shortcut through the woods to our house. It certainly didn't take long for those two big dogs to find Triangle's trail. The very minute their long noses smelled it they started acting almost crazy. We could hardly keep up with them, they went so fast. They almost dragged Big Jim and Circus, with Little Jim and Poetry and me following along behind.

Away we went, out across our orchard and through a hole in the fence where there was some hair caught in the wires—maybe because Triangle's sides were so fat, I thought—across the road and straight for Sugar Creek where all of a sudden the trail was lost.

Say! Those two big hounds with their tails whirling like they were trying to crank a couple of old-fashioned automobiles and with their noses close to the ground, whined and acted worried and ran up and down the creek like they'd lost the trail and couldn't find it.

"I'll bet Triangle jumped in the creek to get the bees off him," Poetry said.

And Little Jim said, "M-m-maybe he got drowned!"

But Circus said, "He'd be so fat with all that honey in him that he'd float—like Poetry."

And Poetry said, making up a poem:

"A little round bear with a little round
tummy,
That sank when he swam like a tub full
of honey."

It was funny but for some reason none of us laughed.

The dogs kept running up and down the creek, dragging Circus and Big Jim after them. Then all of a sudden one of them let out a long, high-pitched bawl which meant he'd found the trail again. We all ran as fast as we could to where he'd found it and there as plain as day was a bear's track, a whole lot of them, in fact, right there in the cool mud. I remembered from the books I'd read in Dad's library that bears actually plaster clay on their noses and faces when they get stung by bees, so it won't hurt so much and will get well quicker.

Right away we were running again, following the dogs along the bank of Sugar Creek, right past the old swimming hole and through the swamp, straight for the hills.

Those big long-voiced dogs acted more and more excited all the time, like the track was getting what Circus called "hot," which meant we were about to catch up with the bear.

"I'll bet Triangle went up to Old Man Paddler's cabin," Little Jim puffed beside me. I was thinking the same thing because we'd all been up there with him two or three times during the summer. In fact, that's where Old Man Paddler had showed Little Jim how to teach Triangle his tricks, and the old man had fed Triangle a nice fat mouse he had caught the night before in a trap. There are always mice around any cabin that is built in the woods. Every time we'd taken Triangle up there Old Man Paddler had had a mouse to give him.

When we were going through the swamp, the dogs lost their trail for a minute, and Little Jim happened to remember it was Sunday and he wondered if it would be all right for us to go hunting on Sunday because our gang didn't do a lot of things that other people did on Sundays. But Poetry remembered a Bible verse that said it was all right to help a sheep get out of the ditch if it fell in on the Sabbath. And Little Jim said, "Does it say anything about a *bear* being *lost,* and that it's all right to look for him with dogs?"

We all decided that if it was all right to help get a sheep out of a ditch on the Sabbath, it would be all right to help save a little bear's life, so when the dogs found the trail again we hurried right along after them.

Sure enough, Triangle had gone to Old Man Paddler's cabin. Maybe he knew that with all the honey in him, he'd need some meat quick so he wouldn't get too sick, and he had thought of how good a nice fat mouse would taste, just like a boy wants a slice of bread and butter when he's had too much candy. Pretty soon the dogs were there, their tails whirling and their voices sounding like a baby taking a walk across the keys of the organ in our church.

In a minute the door opened and Old Man Paddler was there standing in the doorway with his long white whiskers covering most of his chest. He took off his heavy glasses so he could see us better because he only used them when he wanted to see something up close, such as when he read or ate or something.

Circus made the dogs quit barking and the old man said, "Well, well, where's Dragonfly?" He knew us all by name and he even called us by our nicknames, which made us know he liked us. And it helped us to like him even better.

"Dragonfly went to visit his cousin," Poetry said.

Then the old man threw back his fine old white head and laughed and said, "It seems like a good day for visitors. If you boys will tie up your dogs and come in, I'll let you see my company, but be very quiet because this is a hospital now."

Pretty soon we were all in the main room of the cabin. It took a minute for our eyes to get adjusted so we could see clearly. I looked around and there was the cook stove, a table, three or four chairs, a nice clean cot over in the corner, and a great big high rick of wood along the wall which my dad and some men had helped cut last summer and which the Sugar Creek Gang had carried into the cabin ourselves so there'd be plenty of firewood for the next winter which would be coming soon.

Then I saw the big stone fireplace, and there, right in the middle of it, was Triangle lying very quiet and breathing hard like he was pretty sick. There was clay packed on his nose and face and his fat little sides were sticking out like he had eaten even more than twenty pounds of honey.

Little Jim was so tickled he almost screamed, and he started to jump right down and hug Triangle he was so glad to see him again, but the old man stopped him, saying, "He's very cross now, because he is sick but he'll get well in a few days, and then you may play with him again. I'll nurse him back to health as soon as I can. I'll give him plenty of medicine, but I think you'd better leave him right here with me until he is well."

"What kind of medicine?" Little Jim wanted to know.

"Nature's medicine," the old man said, "just good sweet milk and plenty of fresh meat, and *no* honey or syrup or candy. Maybe you boys can arrange with your folks to bring up milk and meat everyday for awhile."

So that was the way we got Little Jim's bear back, and we were all happy again.

5

WELL, WINTER was getting ready to come out of
the north to visit us. School was on in full swing
and we were all busy with lessons and examina-
tions and hard study, and of course a lot of good
hard play too. Nothing very important happened
for awhile until Big Jim and Big Bob Till got
into a fierce fight in which Big Jim almost got
licked, and maybe would have if— But let me
tell you about it just like it happened.

It happened on the way home from school one
afternoon and it was all on account of Big Bob
Till saying some rough words to a new girl who
had moved into our neighborhood and was going
to our school. As I told you, we had a new minister in our church and she was his daughter and
was almost as good a Christian as Little Jim. And
she wasn't stuck up like some girls are.

Like most boys, none of our gang liked girls
very well although we kinda knew they belonged
to the human race. And I realized we ought to
be kind to them because my mom had been a

girl once herself, and if my mom had been one, then girls must be all right.

The new girl was named Sylvia and she was in the eighth grade and was very smart. She had curly brown hair that hung down in the back of her neck and was all tucked inside of something that looked kinda like a yellow fish net, and was called a "snood." Sylvia was the first girl in our school to wear one because they were just beginning to be in style.

I could see right away that Big Jim thought Sylvia was pretty nice, even though he wasn't old enough to, because after she started coming to our school I noticed Big Jim combed his hair a little straighter. And when we played prisoner's base, he tried especially hard not to let her be a prisoner very long.

Big Bob Till, who, as I told you, is Tom Till's brother, must have noticed Big Jim being especially courteous to Sylvia, and he didn't like it. He must have had an awful dirty mind, for his words about half the time were even worse than his father's were. He was always telling bad things about girls, which filthy-minded boys and men often do. None of our gang ever talked like that, not only because Big Jim wouldn't stand for it but because we had sense enough not to. We wouldn't even let anybody else do it when they were with us. In fact, I had a hard time to keep from punching a boy in the nose whenever

43

I heard him using dirty words. As I may have told you once before, all our gang were Christians and we weren't ashamed of it, and we felt sorry for any boy who was afraid to be one for fear some ignorant person would make fun of him. It's silly to be afraid to be a Christian.

Say! Do you know what? If they burned people up alive now like they used to hundreds of years ago because they were Christians, and if they decided to burn up the Sugar Creek Gang, I'll bet Little Jim would stand there looking at the great big yellow flames of fire just before they put him in. And even though he might be scared almost to death, he'd start to sing one of his favorite songs:

Dare to be a Daniel, dare to stand alone,
Dare to have a purpose true, dare to make it known.

Then if he had to, for Jesus' sake, he'd say, "All right! Put me into that old fire, if you want to! I won't deny Jesus!"

Well, when school was out that afternoon, all of the seventeen pupils came scrambling out the only door the little red brick schoolhouse had, coming out and scattering kinda like the tiny bird shot out of my dad's big shot gun, or maybe like honey bees crawling out of a hive and then flying away.

Our teacher had a rule that there wasn't to be

44

any fighting on the way home from school, and all boys had to be courteous to girls.

Well, Sylvia and her little sister Jeanelle, who was in the third grade, lived farther away from school than any of the rest of us, about a mile up the road from our house. There weren't any school buses like some rural schools have, so sometimes their parents would come and get them in their car, especially if it was a rainy day. All our gang always walked home together as far as we could, wrestling and walking on top of the rail fences and acting like frisky young colts after they had been shut up in a barn all day. Sometimes we'd take a shortcut through the woods so we could be together a little longer.

When we went down Poetry's lane, Big Jim and Circus could walk almost all the way home with Poetry and me. Then they could climb over the fence and go through the woods and get home just as quick. Sylvia and her sister Jeanelle had to walk home on the same little road we did. It seemed that Big Jim walked with Poetry and me nearly every night since Sylvia had started coming to our school. Of course we didn't all walk in one bunch like geese or ducks do when they're going some place but were all strung out, boys walking with boys and girls with girls.

That afternoon we were walking along, Poetry and Big Jim and all the gang, with Sylvia and Jeanelle and Circus' kinda ordinary-looking sister whom I was going to kill a spider for if I got a chance. It wasn't because I liked Circus' sister, like I thought Big Jim did Sylvia, but because there was something inside of me that made me want to be kind to some girl. Her name was Lucille, which wasn't a bad name. She was wearing a snood that day too and had her hair all tucked inside nice and neat like Sylvia's.

While I was walking along beside Poetry and Big Jim, carrying my lunch bucket, I kept wishing that I would start running as fast as I could and turn a handspring in the grass like Circus was doing right that minute, but I knew I'd make a fizzle of it and maybe get my nose bumped.

Then I got to thinking what if some boy would run real fast and grab Lucille's snood and throw it away so I could run and catch him and give him a licking and give the snood back to her, so she'd smile back at me when I grinned at her sometime across the schoolroom when I wasn't supposed to.

While I was thinking that, all of a sudden Big Bob Till, who had had to stay in after school because he'd done or said something he shouldn't have, came running down the lane, leaping and yelling. He whizzed right past us boys and made a beeline for Sylvia. Before I could even guess what he was going to do, he had snatched off her snood and had thrown it over the fence where it landed out in the cornfield. Then he called out to her roughly, "Old smarty! There goes your snood and all your brains with it! I wouldn't have *had* to stay in after school if you hadn't told on me!"

Sylvia's hands reached for her hair and tried to untangle it, and she said to Bob in a dignified voice, "I didn't tell Miss Mulder anything, although someone should have. Such language! A gentleman wouldn't say such things as you said to me today!"

Sylvia had a kinda contralto voice that sounded like her mother had given her good training. Last Sunday she had sung a solo in our church and it had sounded very pretty. The words were:

What a wonderful, wonderful Saviour,
Who would die on the cross for me!

Then her father, who as I told you was our new minister, had preached a swell sermon about a man named Lazarus being raised from the dead. Lazarus was buried in a grave that was just like a cave, and there was a great big stone rolled against the mouth of the cave. Some of Jesus' friends had rolled the big rock away and, just as soon as Jesus called Lazarus by name and told him to come out, all of a sudden there he was, alive and well. Just think of it! And he'd been dead for four days!

Well, Lazarus was still all wrapped up in his grave clothes, so Jesus said to his friends, "Loose him and let him go!" which they did.

Well, I thought Sylvia was right. Certainly no gentleman would say and do what Big Bob Till had done. I guess Big Jim was thinking the same thing, only his thoughts must have been boiling hot. When he saw that pretty, yellow snood go sailing over the fence into the cornfield, he stopped dead still. His jaw clicked shut and his fists doubled up, and I knew from the way I'd felt at different times in my life that something was going to happen.

And it did! Just then Big Bob Till said something to Sylvia even worse than he had said to her on the school ground that day. The next thing I knew I was holding Big Jim's lunch bucket in one hand and mine in the other, and Big Jim was shooting like an arrow straight for that big foul-mouthed bully.

Say, Big Bob Till must have been expecting something like that. I suppose he hadn't forgotten the way Big Jim had licked the daylights out of him last summer on Bumblebee Hill and maybe he'd been planning to get revenge. He knew a lot of wrestling tricks too. He whirled around and stooped low just as Big Jim got there. He grabbed Big Jim around the knees with his arms, turned a backward somersault, and threw him clear over his head.

Big Jim landed with a thud flat on his back in the grass. And before you could say Gingerbernooster, Bob was on top of him slamming him with his fists and yelling, "You fuzzy-mustached, church-going sissy! You're going to get—" Then Bob swore terribly, using the same words his father does when *he* swears.

Little Jim beside me was as white as a sheet almost. Little Jeanelle was crying. Lucille looked scared. And Sylvia stood looking kinda like a queen that had lost her crown.

With the two lunch buckets in my hands, I must have felt like little red-haired David in the Bible did when he was supposed to fight with Saul's armor on. A great big giant was about to kill him. And he was used to having only a sling shot. I kept wondering why Big Jim didn't turn over and shove that bully off him and fight like I knew Big Jim could. Then I noticed that he had turned pale like he was sick. Then I heard him groan and I knew he was already licked and if somebody didn't help him, maybe Bob's hard fists would break his nose or something.

Say, it didn't take me long to get rid of those lunch buckets. I didn't even take time to see where they fell. I made a flying tackle for one of Bob's legs, got hold of it, shut my eyes, and held on for dear life. I started pulling and yanking and twisting. Whenever I heard Big Jim groan, I felt myself getting madder because I could still hear Bob's fists whamming away at him.

In another jiffy Poetry and Circus were in the fight too, and somebody else. A little later when we got ourselves untangled, what do you suppose we found out? At first I couldn't believe my eyes, but the reason it had been so easy to pull Bob Till off Big Jim was not only because Poetry and Circus had helped but because Little Tom had gotten ahold of his brother's other leg and was fighting on our side!

We had Bob down on his stomach with Poetry sprawled across his shoulders, and the rest of us holding his arms and legs. There on the ground beside us was Big Jim, with Little Jim and Dragonfly trying to help him sit up. You see, when Big Jim had landed on his back there had been a rock there about two inches in diameter and it had hurt his back so much he hadn't been able to fight at all.

In a minute Little Tom Till got up and climbed over the fence and got Sylvia's snood which he found hanging on an ear of corn about halfway up the stalk. He came back and handed it to Sylvia kinda bashful-like, without looking up, so he didn't see her smile. But we all heard her say, "Thank you, Tom. You're a gentleman." And I wished I'd been Tom myself. From that minute on, I knew Tom and I were going to be good friends and maybe he'd belong to the Sugar Creek Gang someday.

6

WE DIDN'T DARE let Bob up because he was still angry and might do something desperate, so we kept on holding him down. It was especially easy because there were so many of us.

It was hard for Poetry to stay angry very long. Nearly everything anybody said or did reminded him of a poem. So while he was still holding Bob's shoulders down, he kinda lifted his head and saw all of us boys with our arms and legs all tangled up. It must have made him think of a centipede which is a many-legged insect, so he began to quote:

> "A centipede was happy quite
> Until a frog, in fun,
> Said, 'Pray, which leg comes after which?'
> This roused his mind to such a pitch,
> He lay distracted in the ditch,
> Considering how to run."

Bob Till, lying there in the ditch, *did* have a lot of legs on him only they were boys' legs and they weren't all his own. He had Poetry's, mine, his own, Tom's, and Circus' which is ten, and if you counted each arm for a leg, that'd make twenty.

Well, we had to do something with our centipede, so we decided to ask Big Jim. Big Jim still looked kinda pale. He struggled to his feet and stood looking down at us like he thought we were worth a million dollars. Then he turned to Sylvia who had her snood on again and said, "He's your prisoner, Sylvia. What shall we do with him?"

I don't know what I expected her to say, but I thought he ought to have some kind of punishment, such as being thrown into Sugar Creek with his clothes on.

Sylvia really looked like a queen, now that she had her crown again, and I felt proud that Big Jim liked her. Someday we might even decide to let her belong to our gang, I thought, and Big Jim could be the king and she the queen.

As I told you before, Sylvia was our new minister's daughter, and she not only got good grades in school but if the church would give grades for the ones that were the best Christians, she would have had "A" in everything, which is the highest grade you can get.

Sylvia stood there in the lane with the September wind blowing some of her hair across her forehead and she said—and I guess she must have heard her dad say it first—she said, "Bob doesn't need to be punished. He needs to be changed." Her voice was so kind it sounded like she was sorry for him.

Bob squirmed and begged us to let him up so he could breathe, so we made Poetry get off his shoulders but we wouldn't let him up yet.

Do you know what Sylvia decided to do with Bob? I guess she knew that his dad was an infidel and that Bob had never been to church or Sunday school in his life, so she decided that now would be as good a time as any for him to hear his first sermon.

When Little Jim knew what was going to happen, his eyes got all shiny. Circus' monkey face looked kinda like Sugar Creek's face does when there isn't any wind. Big Jim's eyes were looking at Sylvia.

Say, that was the grandest church service I ever went to in my life, even if it did last only seven or eight minutes. We didn't have any piano or organ or hymnbooks or any choir, and nobody said "Amen" out loud. But I kept thinking all the time, "Atta girl, Sylvia!" which is about the same as amen only it isn't quite as reverent, and people don't say it in church. But I'll bet Jesus knew what I was thinking and was glad.

We had flowers though, like churches generally have on their altars. All along the rail fencerow were beautiful goldenrod that sorta nodded their heads in the wind every now and then like they were saying the same thing I was thinking.

If you take a look at a goldenrod up real close, it kinda looks like the chandelier that hangs from the ceiling in the middle of our church, with maybe eight or ten different lights fastened to one stem. Only the goldenrod doesn't hang down but holds its head up toward the sky, like Sylvia's dad says Christians can do when their sins are all forgiven.

While Sylvia was talking, a whole flock of noisy blackbirds came flying across the cornfield and started holding a convention or a revival meeting or something in the old hickory tree across the road. They made me think of the winged black notes on Little Jim's music sheets—so we had music even if it was kinda out of tune.

Pretty soon the blackbirds got so noisy with their wheezy voices that we couldn't hear Sylvia very well, so that broke up our meeting. But not till after Bob had heard enough to know that he was lost and could be saved if he wanted to, only he would have to repent of his sins and believe that Jesus Christ had come out of the grave after He had died for all our sins and was alive now and would come into any boy's heart if he wanted Him to.

When Sylvia finished telling Bob what everybody in the world ought to know, she said to us, "Loose him and let him go," which we did.

Say, the minute Big Bob was free, he looked around like he couldn't see very well, and I thought I saw a tear trying to get out of one of his eyes, kinda like the moon trying get out from behind a big black cloud. In a jiffy he was on his feet and over the fence and running toward home without saying a word. I guess maybe he was pretty surprised that we didn't give him some awful hard punishment. I decided maybe he was in a hurry to get away, so just in case the tear got bigger and fell out of his eye, it would fall where nobody could see it.

When I got home that afternoon a little later than usual, I set my lunch bucket on our kitchen table, ate a sandwich Mom had left for me, and went out to gather the eggs which was always one of my chores and a lot of fun. One of our old white hens laid her egg in a nest up in our haymow, so I had to climb up there everyday to get it, that is, unless she didn't happen to lay an egg that day. Sometimes hens don't.

When I was up there that afternoon, I got to thinking about the time when I'd tucked my little New Testament in a crack away up in a corner and decided to leave it until Circus' drinking father would get saved. I went up there every day and read it because that was one of my rules, to read it every day.

Well, I thought, if Circus' dad could be saved, then why not Big Bob Till? I tell you it seemed a grand thing to be a Christian since listening to Sylvia's talk. I stood there on a great big pile of alfalfa hay, which cows like so well, and I listened to see if there was anybody downstairs. No one was, anyway not any people. I did hear old Mixy, our black and white cat, mewing like she was lonesome. I took my New Testament out of my pocket and read a very interesting chapter. New Testaments have some places that even grown-ups can't understand without studying them, and my dad has a lot of different books that help to explain them, which is what all boys' parents should have so they can answer all the hard questions that come popping into a boy's head—and just as quick come tumbling out of his mouth.

I finished reading my chapter. Then I climbed up over the hay to the place where the crack was in the log, and there was a spider web right across the crack. Then I put both knees down on the hay and prayed for Bob Till, even if I didn't like him very well. Then I climbed down and went on gathering eggs.

Pretty soon I came to the ladder which leads up, higher and higher, all the way up to a cupola on the tip-top of our barn. I always liked to climb up there and look out the glass windows across the cornfields and up along Sugar Creek. There were a lot of spider webs up there too, so I couldn't help but remember that I'd planned to kill a spider for Lucille Brown, who is Circus' kinda ordinary-looking sister. In fact, she was more than kinda ordinary-looking. Anyway, I decided if I was going to kill a spider for her, I'd better hurry up and do it, or pretty soon it'd be winter and there wouldn't be any spiders to kill.

Well, after supper, while the sun was still up pretty high, Little Jim's mom sent him over to our house on an errand and told him he could stay a while and play with me, and then just before dark, I could ride him home on the back of my bicycle. I asked Dad if we could go down to the spring and get a drink, and he said we could but not to go in swimming, which we didn't want to do anyway.

Pretty soon away we went as fast as we could run, Little Jim running like a little cottontail rabbit and I kinda like a big long-legged jackrabbit. I guess I'd grown about two inches that summer and was beginning to be all hands and feet, which made me look more and more like Bill Collins, which wasn't much. But Little Jim liked me and didn't care how I looked on the outside.

Each of us took a drink of water at the spring, lying down on our stomachs and trying to drink like birds do. They dip their bills in the water and scoop up a billful and then tip their heads up in the air so the water'll run down their throats. They keep their bills moving all the time their heads are up, like they are saying and thinking something cheerful.

Little Jim was lying on the other side of the spring from me and we could see the reflections of our heads in the pool of water, which looked almost like a mirror. That little cottontail rabbit, which I thought would be a good nickname for Little Jim, was always surprising people by saying such wise things. You never could tell what important thoughts might be hiding just behind those two pretty blue eyes of his. All of a sudden he said, "Do you know what the little birds say when they tip their heads up like that when they're drinking?"

And I said, "No. What?"

And he said, "They say, 'Thank You, heavenly Father.'"

I didn't say anything but I liked Little Jim better than ever.

Pretty soon we had our shoes and stockings off, which our parents hadn't said we couldn't do, and waded down along the creek skipping rocks, making old Sugar Creek's face smile or frown, whichever we wanted him to. We'd throw in two stones at once, one a little farther out than the other, to make his eyes; then one in the middle for his nose; then we'd skip another stone, making a big, long water furrow all the way across, for his mouth.

When we were tired of doing that, we decided

to walk past the old swimming hole just to sorta remember the good times we'd had there, and to feel sad because the summer was gone. When we got there we stopped a minute, and all of a sudden we heard somebody coming.

We ducked down behind a bed of wild irises whose flowers had bloomed last summer from May to July. My dad says the iris gets its name from the Greek meaning of the word which is "rainbow," and its flowers do look kinda like rainbows, except there is too much blue. My mom even has some all-white and all-yellow irises in our garden.

Say, Little Jim and I kept as quiet as we could, and I kept my eyes wide open, looking between two long sword-shaped leaves to see who was coming. I couldn't help but think about the time Little Jim's bear had run away, and I wondered who had cut his collar and turned him loose. In fact, right that very minute we were lying in the very spot where Triangle had been tied. Also right that very minute I was feeling something hard in the grass under my elbow. While we were keeping quiet, waiting to see who was coming, I looked to see what the hard thing under my elbow was, and I almost hollered, I was so surprised. For right in front of my astonished eyes, and in my kinda shaky right hand, was a big barlow knife with the blade open. It was rusty like it had been lying there all summer in the sun and rain!

I didn't have time to think because right that second whoever was coming stopped on the other side of the willow from us and began looking around like he was trying to find something.

Little Jim nudged me and my heart started beating fast and even hurting because it was Circus himself! I thought something I shouldn't have thought and couldn't help it. I thought what if it was Circus who had cut the little bear loose, and had lost his knife there and was looking for it now? But that idea was silly because Circus had been in swimming with us at the time. Or what if it had been Circus' dad who used to drink and be a bad man before he was saved? What if that day last summer he had planned to steal Triangle and sell him, and then had heard us coming and had had to get away quick? But I didn't like to think that either because when a man really gets saved, he isn't a bad man anymore and he doesn't get drunk or steal or swear or be mean to his family.

We couldn't do anything but lie still and wait, not being able to see very well now because Circus was on the other side of the big willow shrub. Pretty soon Circus took off his old straw hat and shinned himself up a little elm tree. Say, I never saw a boy that could climb a tree so fast in my life. The next thing I knew, he was stand-

ing up on a limb with his back to us, and what
do you think he did up there? I couldn't believe
my ears at first, but I had to. Circus began to
sing. Think of it! *Sing!* And the song he was
singing was one of the songs in our hymnbook
at church.

I looked at Little Jim and he looked at me and
his eyes were shining like he was very proud of
Circus. It was the first time I'd heard Circus sing
by himself. He usually sang with some of our
gang sitting beside him in church, with maybe
Poetry's squawky voice growling along beside
him to sorta keep anybody from hearing how
good Circus' voice really was. His voice was almost as pretty as a meadowlark's, which is as
clear as a flute.

Well, Circus stood up there in the top of
that little swaying elm sapling, maybe imagining
he was standing before a big crowd, and singing. His high soprano just quavered out across
the creek like an owl's voice does at night.

I felt something inside of me pushing its way
up into my throat like a whole bucketful of tears
were coming up out of an old-fashioned well, and
I swallowed it down quick 'cause I knew that if
that whole bucketful of tears got up as high as
my eyes, it'd spill over.

The song Circus was singing was Dragonfly's
favorite song and I wished he'd been there to
hear it. I'll write down only the first verse for

you, 'cause I suppose nearly every boy or girl who goes to Sunday school or church knows it. It starts like this:

> I will sing the wondrous story,
> Of the Christ who died for me,
> How he left his home in glory,
> For the cross of Calvary.

Little Jim reached his round little brown hand over to me and nudged me and whispered, "It's going to be a surprise for church tomorrow morning. My mother is teaching Circus to sing it." Little Jim's mother was a wonderful musician and our church pianist.

You see Sylvia's father found out right away that Circus had a good voice, so he decided to put it to work because anybody that has a good voice ought to use it and not let it get rusty like an old knife that's been lost.

Well, I had that rusty-bladed knife in my pocket right that minute, and I was wondering whose it was, even while I was listening to Circus sing.

Little Jim and I began to feel just then that we'd better go away 'cause Circus was just practicing and he wouldn't want anybody to listen to him, so we sneaked along through the bushes and the tall weeds toward the spring. While we were walking along I got to thinking about a story in my *Child's Story Bible* which tells about a man named Moses who saw a bush on fire once which wasn't burning up because God Himself was right in the middle of it. God's big kind voice called to Moses and said for him to take off his shoes because the ground he was standing on was holy ground. It was holy because God was there. Of course, I was already barefoot and couldn't take mine off. But I'll bet I felt like Moses did anyway.

Say, my dad says there isn't any scientist in the world who can explain why the sun doesn't burn up. There is something in it that makes it keep on just like it is, all the time, just like the burning bush in the Bible story. And if there wasn't any sun, we'd all freeze to death quick, so it's silly to be an infidel like John Till who couldn't even live a minute himself if it wasn't for God keeping him alive.

Say, there was more than one surprise for the people in our church the next Sunday morning. I guess Sylvia's dad knew and liked boys even better than our other minister had. He must have thought boys were important because he made us feel like he needed us. Anyway just before Circus sang his solo, Mr. Johnson, that being our minister's last name, made a fine talk about boys, saying that even all the great men in the world had had to be boys first whether they wanted to or not. Would you believe it? He had Little Jim come up to the platform and tell us a short story just like teachers do in school, and this is what Little Jim said:

"Once upon a time in a wicked old saloon there was a man named Peter Bilhorn who made his living playing the piano for the men who bought and drank their whiskey there. One night while Peter was sitting at the piano in that smoky old room, some YMCA workers came in and gave him a piece of paper called a tract that had the gospel printed on it, and Peter got mad and tore it up. They gave him another tract and he was still madder and he tore that one up too. Then they gave him another and he folded it up and put it in his pocket, 'cause he had had a good Christian mother who wanted him to be saved and who had prayed for him. Then Peter went to a special meeting and let Jesus come into his heart, and after that he became a famous song writer and he wrote the song called, "I Will Sing the Wondrous Story.' "

When Little Jim finished his true story, he stood there kinda like a little chipmunk when it is standing up on a stump along Sugar Creek just before it makes a dive for the ground and goes whisking away somewhere. Then Little Jim, with his blue eyes looking as innocent as Charlotte Ann's do, came back to our row, squeezed his way past my mom and my dad who had Charlotte Ann on his lap, and sat down beside me. Say that little fellow was trembling like a scared little baby rabbit in a boy's hand, but he was happy.

In a half minute we were all listening to Circus sing that very same song while Little Jim's mom, who had a new fall hat on that looked like a small sunflower upside down, played the piano for him.

Little Tom Till was sitting on the other side of me, with one eye swollen a little bit like he'd been in another fight. It made me feel all clean inside when I thought about how I'd invited him to come to church the first time, and he actually seemed to like to come.

After church and just before we went home while we were out under a big locust tree on our church lawn, I asked Tom where he got his black eye, knowing I hadn't done it this time. At first he didn't want to tell me. Then he looked around to be sure nobody else could hear, and he said, "Bob gave it to me for fighting on your side after school Friday." And I knew the Sugar Creek Gang was going to have still more trouble with the oldest Till boy.

Just then I happened to think about the knife I'd found, so I took it out of my pocket and started to scrape the edge of one of my fingernails when Little Tom said, surprised, "Where'd you get that knife?" and I said, "Oh nowhere, I just found it!"

"Let me see it," he said, just as Poetry came over to where we were.

Tom held the knife in his hand awhile, turning it over and over, and looking kinda queer, then he said, "See that little nick in the handle?" and I said, "Yes."

And he said, "I'll bet it's the one Bob lost 'cause his had a nick in the same place."

That made it look more than ever like Bob Till had been the one who'd cut Triangle's collar that day.

7

FALL WAS COMING FAST, and all the birds that had gotten married in the spring and their little baby birds that had grown up began to gather in flocks, like boys do in gangs, only some of them weren't so noisy and they didn't turn somersaults or walk on their hands, which they didn't have anyway. Blackbirds gathered in one flock, sparrows in another, and crows in another. Say! as soon as the leaves had begun to fall from the trees, about a thousand crows gathered in our woods, and I never heard such noise as when their hoarse old voices cawed and scolded all day long and flew around from one place to another and back again and up and down from the trees to the ground, scolding all the time.

There had been a family of swallows in our garage which had had their nest on a tie beam. You know, a pair of swallows sometimes have two or three broods of baby birds in one summer in the same nest. Ours had quadruplets the first time, quintuplets the second, and sextuplets the third, making fifteen new swallow children in one summer! But when fall started to come they were all gone, and I suppose they joined with a lot of others that were flying up and down Sugar Creek just above the water, up and down, crossing and criss-crossing, their tails forked like the fork of a boy's slingshot.

I knew that old Jack Frost, who isn't a real person, would come pretty soon and he'd kill all our garden stuff, and after that old grandpa winter himself would come with his snowy white whiskers and it'd be terribly cold. Say! That reminds me of Old Man Paddler whose life our gang saved once and who had told us that someday when he died there'd be something for each one of us in his will. And that reminds me that pretty soon in this story, just as soon as I get to it, I'd better keep my promise which I made in my story *We Killed a Bear* and tell you what happened that winter on a cold — *very* cold — day when our gang went up to see Old Man Paddler.

Fall comes before winter though. In the fall, Jack Frost paints all the leaves in the woods yellow, gold, and red, and he kills all the flowers and garden things. Pretty soon there wouldn't be any butterflies or caterpillars or spiders. Well, I got to thinking it was time I killed that spider I'd planned to. At last one day I got a chance, although I hadn't planned on nearly everybody in our school being present when it happened, and I certainly hate to tell you what *did* happen, but I suppose you'll want to know — or do you?

You see, the idea first came to me away back in the middle of that summer when Little Jim picked up a baby bird that had fallen out of its nest and had very carefully put it back in. He had wrapped his handkerchief around it first so the old mother bird wouldn't smell where his hand had touched it and maybe kill it, like some mother birds do when a boy's hands have handled their babies. That's why a boy ought not to take a baby bird out of its nest and play with it.

Well, when that fuzzy, scrawny, kinda bulgy-eyed, big mouthed cute little baby bird was in its nest again beside its little brothers and sisters, Little Jim and I watched them a few minutes while the old mother bird and her husband and all the neighbor birds scolded in the trees and bushes all around us. Then we went away. And I thought of Charlotte Ann who was even more helpless than a baby bird and I thought I ought to be very kind to her. Then I thought that a boy ought to be kind to all girls who are such helpless things and are afraid of mice and spiders and worms and June-bugs and caterpillars and centipedes.

So when school started and I saw that Big Jim was especially kind to Sylvia, I knew it'd be all right for me to be especially courteous to Circus' kinda ordinary-looking sister, Lucille, who, when she was wearing a blue hair ribbon, didn't look so ordinary—although she didn't exactly act as helpless as a baby bird, and I'd never heard her scream when she saw an ugly caterpillar crawling toward her.

It happened at school one day when we were sitting out behind the woodshed at noon, eating our lunch. Sylvia and another girl and Lucille were sitting with each other on one end of a long log, and Poetry and Dragonfly and I were sitting on the other end, with about three feet between me and Lucille. I had two apples in my lunch bucket and all of a sudden I thought of the baby bird Little Jim had put back in the nest, and how helpless it was, and how mother birds bring worms and caterpillars and things and feed their bird babies. That made me think of how girls are afraid of caterpillars and spiders. So when nobody was looking, I slipped my reddest, shiniest apple over into Lucille's lunch basket. Say, she smiled just like Charlotte Ann does when Mom gives her a bite of spinach which she likes very much. Then her face turned redder than our old red rooster's comb had been before he got killed. I kept on eating a banana I had just peeled and talking to Poetry when all of a sudden Big Bob Till came walking past, swinging a baseball bat. He stopped and looked at Dragonfly and Poetry and me and said to us, "Will you girls hurry up and get through eating so we can play ball?"

Say! It didn't take me even a tenth of a minute to get angry at being called a girl because I didn't like girls and wouldn't *be* one for a million dollars, so I shouted to Big Bob Till to go and tend to his own business. With Lucille sitting beside me, not more than three feet away, I even felt big enough to give Big Bob a licking.

"My business," Bob Till said sarcastically, "is to upset the log you're sitting on!" And with that remark he swooped down, shoved his baseball bat under the log and gave a mighty heave. And over went the log and three boys and three girls and six lunch buckets each one going in six different directions.

And! Out from under the log scrambled a great big, long-legged brown spider that started straight toward Lucille!

As mad as I was, I didn't forget what I wanted to do. Lucille saw the spider at the same time I did, but she didn't act a bit scared. So I grabbed a stick and started yelling, "Look out, Lucille! There's a spider! *It'll bite you!*"

You see, I thought if I could get her really scared, I'd seem more like a hero to her, when I killed the spider, so I yelled again, still louder, "Lucille! Quick! Get out of the way! There's a great big ugly, longlegged spider about to eat you up!"

Well, this is the part of the story I hate to tell anybody, but I may as well get it over with. That helpless girl grabbed the stick out of my hand, which was Little Jim's stick anyway, and quicker than a dog can bark, she swooped down on that spider and whacked it with the stick and jumped on it with her shoes and killed it herself! Then she looked at me, disgusted, and said "Fraidy cat! What is there about a dumb old spider to be afraid of! Did you think it was goin' to bite you?"

Then Lucille threw the stick across the schoolyard, and she and Sylvia and the other girl swished around, gathered up their scattered lunch buckets, and went in the schoolhouse.

After that I was more disgusted with girls than ever, and for some reason I didn't like Bill Collins very well either, not for a long time.

8

PRETTY SOON it was winter. Winter in our country meant a lot of snow and plenty of wind. Snowdrifts were sometimes higher than our heads. We made snow forts in our school yard and had real snow battles, all in fun. We even got my little coaster wagon and made a sort of armored tank out of it which we filled full of snowball cannon and bombs, and we charged on each other like modern armies. Only we didn't like to play war very well because real war is so terrible and so many people get killed or have to leave their homes.

We decided to quit playing war so we played other snow games, such as fox and geese. We made snowmen and snow caves and had a lot of fun. Of course we did our chores at night, and I kept right on helping Mom with the dishes at different times. I kept on learning to hang up my clothes on a hanger and always to wipe off my shoes on a mat outside the door or take off my rubbers before I went into the house, so our house would look like a house instead of a barn.

All the time Charlotte Ann kept growing fatter and prettier and Dad kept doing all kinds of antics to get her to smile, such as making funny faces, tickling her chin or cheeks or pink toes, or twisting his big bushy blackish-red eyebrows. In November when she was six months old, two little white baby teeth stuck their edges up through the lower gums of her mouth.

Say, was she ever cross and fussy while those teeth were pushing through! I was as disgusted as anything until Mom reminded me that I'd been even crosser when I was little. I was surprised when I heard that and I didn't like to believe it. I couldn't even remember it but Dad said it was true, so after I'd frowned awhile I quit and forgave Charlotte Ann.

"Charlotte Ann's two teeth came through just in time for our Thanksgiving dinner, only of course she couldn't have any turkey because babies don't eat anything but milk and maybe some ground-up, cooked spinach or whatever a doctor says to feed them.

That was one of the best dinners I ever had in my life and I liked it especially well because we invited Old Man Paddler to eat with us. My red-haried, very freckled faced city cousin was there too. His dad was my dad's brother. They brought with them their tan-brown Aire-

74

dale dog Fritz, who was about medium sized and had thick, rough hair, which looked like it had never been combed, and short ears.

I could see right away that Fritz and our old black and white Mixy cat didn't like each other and I knew there'd be trouble before the visit was over. Fritz didn't like cats very well, which most dogs don't.

As I told you, it was the funniest thing the way I killed our old Thanksgiving turkey—funnier even than the way Dad killed our old red rooster that summer. You know Dad had to kill old Red Comb because he didn't get out of the way when I threw a rock at him, and his leg got broken. I'd better tell you about that before I explain about the turkey.

You see, Dad came out of the house just about a minute after I'd thrown the rock. And seeing old Red Comb flopping around like he was on crutches, he ran and caught him. Just as soon as Dad knew Red Comb's leg was broken and I had confessed I'd done it, but not exactly on purpose, he swung old Red Comb up, caught his big hand around his neck and whirled him around and around maybe seven or eight times like he was turning the handle of a grindstone real fast. Quicker than the shake of a lamb's tail, old Red Comb was on the ground, flopping without any head, which was in Dad's hand.

Then while old Red Comb finished dying,

Dad gave me a good licking with a willow switch which I'd carried home one day and left there by our woodpile. Afterward, when the licking had quit hurting and I was a good boy again, I decided that was one of the reasons I liked my mom and dad so well: They wouldn't let me think it was all right to do anything wrong.

Well, the day before Thanksgiving, my red-haired, very freckled faced city cousin and I went out to the fenced pen where our big fat old turkey was locked up, getting fatter and lazier all the time. Fritz, their Airedale dog, was with us. His gay tail was standing straight up like the tail of the little blue Scotch terrier on Charlotte Ann's bassinet.

Dogs, you know, have at least eight different kinds of tails. There is a book in my library which tells about them. You see my parents had a little corner of our library filled with books especially for boys, and I called it *my* library. There was a book on wild animals of America, birds of America, wild flowers, trees, and a big very beautiful *Child's Story Bible* which was easy to read and understand, and many good storybooks. I guess my parents thought my mind was as important as the rest of me, and they wanted to give it something to eat. They knew it was especially good for a boy to read good books.

One of these books was called a "fact" book, and it had a short chapter telling all about the

76

different kinds of dogs' tails. The "ring" tail starts straight up, then curves around over the dog's back, making a complete circle. The "sickle" tail is shaped like the little sharp sickle Dad uses to cut weeds. The "whip" tail hangs straight back like the tail of Circus' English Setter dog. The "crank" tail hangs like the crank on an automobile. The "gay" tail stands straight up like Fritz's did and like the tails of Scotch terriers do.

When it rained, our old turkey's tail would hang down so the rain would run off his back. When he felt proud and liked to show off, he would spread his feathers up and around like a big fan and he could make himself look almost twice as big as he was.

Well, Walford, which is my city cousin's name, and Fritz and I were standing looking through the wire fence at Caesar, which was our turkey's name. We said different things about him and tried to get him to pay attention to us, which he wouldn't. But once in awhile when he lifted his big naked reddish head and let out a hideous, "Gobble-gobble-obble-obble-obble!" that made Fritz whimper and try to get through the fence so he could play with Caesar.

I was feeling kinda sad 'cause I knew that this time tomorrow old Caesar would be naked all over and without any head or feet and would be lying upside down all full of stuffing in Mom's big oven, getting nice and brown for our dinner. I liked old Caesar and I think he liked me, and sometimes he would let me pet him.

Everything would have been all right if Walford hadn't been so proud of the different tricks Fritz could do. Pretty soon Walford got tired of just looking at old Caesar so he decided he wanted to tie a rope around Caesar's scrawny neck and teach Fritz to lead him. I knew right away that it wasn't a good idea, but Walford didn't know it and neither did Fritz. I argued against it for awhile and then finally gave in and went and got a rope just to show Wally he was wrong.

Then we went into the big thirty-foot pen and I fastened one end of the rope to Caesar's neck while he kept shaking his simpish looking head at me, not liking it very well. Wally fastened the other end of the rope to Fritz's collar.

It turned out that Wally was right. Fritz was as proud as anything, and with a little coaxing, with Wally leading him, he marched around and round the fence, leading old Caesar. I even wished I could get on Caesar's back and ride.

Wally laughed and laughed and shouted, "See there! What did I tell you!"

Yes, Wally was right—that is, for about five minutes, until Fritz spied our old Mixy cat on the other side of the gate, which was shut but wasn't hooked. Something inside of me went first cold and then hot. I seemed to know something was going to happen. In fact it was already happening right before my scared eyes. The very second that that tan-brown airedale spied Mixy's black and white fur there by the gate, he forgot all about being tied to a turkey's neck. He whirled around and made a dash for the gate where I was standing, shoved it open before I could stop him, and gave chase to Mixy—and old Caesar came squawking and gobbling and flopping after him. Wally and I screamed at the top of our lungs for Fritz to stop.

But Fritz was like a car going downhill without any brakes.

I couldn't think very well, but I thought, *What if Fritz catches Mixy? He might even kill her!* I made a grab for the long rope and missed it and fell down right outside the gate.

Then I decided to slam the gate shut, thinking I could catch the rope in the crack between the gate and the post and stop Fritz. I guess I was more worried about saving Mixy than I was Caesar's neck, so without thinking until afterwards, I threw my whole weight against the gate, which was seventy-two pounds, and slammed it shut terribly hard.

Well that stopped Fritz. In fact he stopped so quick he almost turned a somersault backwards. Mixy went scooting like a scared rabbit straight for the barn, flashed through a hole under it, and was safe.

That wasn't all that happened. Believe it or not, that crazy old gate had shut *ker-squash* right on Caesar's scrawny old neck! And it was choking him.

And I—well, if we hadn't had company I suppose I'd have gotten another licking, although my dad was pretty careful not to give me one unless I actually needed it, which wasn't very often anymore.

Anyhow, that's how I killed our old Thanksgiving turkey that fall, although Dad had to finish killing him, which he did with a sharp ax on a big block of wood.

9

POETRY CAME OVER to our house after dinner that day because he'd heard my city cousin was there and he wanted to see Wally. Nearly all our gang had city cousins, and they didn't know very much about country life. In fact, the first time Wally came to see me, which was when he was little, he was so ignorant he thought milk grew in bottles on trees like bananas do.

As I told you, he had a very freckled face. In fact there wasn't even one little tiny corner of his face that didn't have freckles on it. He had two upper front teeth that were too big for such a small face. But that didn't matter because by the time his face quit growing, his teeth would be just the right size. You see the teeth were already as big as they would ever get. Lots of boys—and even girls—look funny when they're ten years old, and they can't help it.

I could see the minute Poetry came wading through the snow toward us that he was in a mischievous mood, and sure enough he was. I'd warned Wally ahead of time not to get angry at anything Poetry did or said. When Poetry got to within about ten feet of us, he stopped and stared at Wally like he was seeing a ghost. Then he stooped and stretched his neck this way and that and rubbed his eyes like he was trying to see better or else like he couldn't believe what he was seeing. He walked clear around us, all the time looking at Wally like he was looking at some interesting animal in a zoo. Then Poetry stopped, grunted, and looked at Wally's freckles and big front teeth that were almost far enough apart to push a feather through and at his red hair which showed under his winter cap. Then with his eyes still on Wally, he said to him, "What big ears you have, Grandma!" quoting from the story of Little Red Riding Hood and the Old Wolf.

Wally's face turned even redder than it was but he didn't get mad. He just grinned and said, in a deep voice like the old wolf's, "All the more to hear you with, my dear."

And Poetry said, "What big teeth you have, Grandma!"

And Wally said, "All the more to eat you up with, my dear!"

With that remark, Wally looked down at Poetry's big feet which certainly were extra large for a boy Poetry's age, and said, "What big feet *you* have, Little Red Riding Hood!" And in a jiffy both boys were in the middle of a good old-fashioned snow fight, neither one of them being angry but each one trying to see which was the strongest, like boys do.

Fritz came running through the snow and joined in the scramble, which reminded me of the turkey. After we'd talked about that awhile, I told Poetry about Old Man Paddler coming to our house for dinner tomorrow. Poetry's eyes lit up at that because every boy that knew Old Man Paddler liked him. I suppose the reason was because Old Man Paddler liked boys and was always doing something for them. Boys are kinda like dogs. If you like them and are kind to them, they'll like you and be kind to you.

Well, that started us all to talking about Old Man Paddler, so Poetry and I had a good time for awhile telling Wally all about the exciting things that had happened to the Sugar Creek Gang that summer. We told him how we'd found a map hidden in a tree and how we had caught a robber at midnight while he was digging for Old Man Paddler's money in a swamp, and different things such as how Little Jim had killed the fierce old mother bear—things like that.

Then kinda like thunder out of a blue sky, Wally asked, "What became of Old Man Paddler's nephew who got shot when the police thought he was a robber?"

We had actually forgotten all about him. In fact, after he'd gotten out of the hospital, he had just disappeared and we hadn't seen or heard of him since.

"He'll get all Old Man Paddler's money, when the old man dies, won't he?" Wally asked.

That made me remember that the kind old man had told the Sugar Creek Gang that he'd put something in his will for every one of us, but that was a secret and nobody else was to know it, so I said to Wally, "I guess Barry Boyland,"—which is the nephew's name—"is the only living relative."

Poetry winked at me secretly and we started talking about something else but not until Wally had said, "I wonder how the old man gets his groceries and things in the winter when the snow is too deep for him to go to town?"

And that's what our gang was wondering that day about the middle of December when we packed Poetry's sled with supplies and went up to see him—but I'll tell you about that in the very next chapter after this one. I'll have to tell you about the Thanksgiving dinner first, when Old Man Paddler ate with us.

Thanksgiving day came at last and we were all sitting around the table at our house: Uncle Phil, Aunt Bessie, Mom, Dad, Charlotte Ann, Wally, me, and dear Old Man Paddler, who had the best table manners I ever saw. He had on his new glasses again, which had the thickest lenses I ever saw, and he always wore them when he was reading or eating and had to see things up real close. Most of the time they were off and in a little brown case in his pocket.

Charlotte Ann was sitting in a high chair, tied in so she wouldn't fall out, and waiting to be fed a bite whenever Mom decided to give one to her. She had on a cute little white dress with a blue and white bib tied on with strings around her neck. There was a blue stripe running all the way down the middle of the bib. Wally and I were both in a very mischievous mood which boys sometimes get into at the wrong times, and not on purpose either.

Just when I was supposed to be quiet because it was time to ask the blessing, I thought of something funny. I felt a smile coming on my face and I knew I was going to snicker out loud, and I wasn't going to be able to help it.

It was Charlotte Ann's blue-and-white bib that caused it, that is, when I looked at Old Man Paddler's long wide white beard that completely covered his chest, making the grandest bib you ever saw and being as clean as Mom's white tablecloth, I thought, *What if he'd accidentally spill some of Mom's blueberry jam on it and it'd run all the way down and make a long blue mark like the blue stripe on Charlotte Ann's bib?*

It wasn't even funny, I guess, but I thought it was, and I snickered out loud just in time to see

Dad's eyebrows drop. In fact, Dad had just said, "Will you ask the blessing first, Bill?"

We nearly always did it that way at our house. I generally prayed a little poem prayer I'd learned. Then Mom or Dad prayed afterward and said something in prose, although we sometimes just bowed our heads and shut our eyes and each one prayed his own prayer quietly without saying any words out loud.

Well, there we all sat with our heads bowed and with Old Man Paddler's white whiskers almost touching my blushing cheeks, and I was supposed to pray!

Things looked bad for me but I knew I hadn't done wrong on purpose and that God knew I was a boy and He liked boys as well as anybody. So I pinched myself hard on the leg so I wouldn't snicker again, and it hurt so much I said ouch instead, and I would have snickered again but I felt Dad's eyebrows hanging over me. So I quoted my little poem prayer:

"We thank Thee, Father, for our homes.
For friends who help each day,
For food we eat and clothes we wear,
For all the gifts Thy children share."

At that very minute I remembered that I'd planned to surprise my parents by adding some words of my own next time I prayed, so I said: "We thank thee also for Jesus, our Saviour, who died for us. And help us to always live for Him. Amen."

Then Old Man Paddler prayed a very beautiful prayer, thanking the Lord for different things such as a country that was free from war and things like that. And would you believe it? That kind old man prayed for all our gang by name, not by our real names either but by the names we had given each other: Big Jim, Little Jim, Circus, Dragonfly, Poetry and Bill, which is me.

When I opened my eyes and looked up, I didn't feel like snickering anymore. I could feel both Mom and Dad looking at me, and I knew they were wondering if I was all right or maybe just a little off in my mind or something.

Old Man Paddler was looking at me with the kindest eyes, as if he liked me very much. I could hardly see his eyes though, unless I looked around the edges of his glasses, on account of the lenses being so thick.

Late that afternoon when I was alone up in our haymow throwing down hay for our horses and cows, I remembered something important my dad had taught me once, and that was that when you know you've done something wrong and you're sorry for it—even if you didn't do it on purpose—if you confess it to God right away, He'll forgive you right that very minute. So while I was standing on a great big bunch of hay, I prayed and told my heavenly Father that

I didn't do it on purpose but I knew it was wrong anyway and that I was sorry.

There wasn't any answer out loud, but I could feel away down inside of me that everything was all right, and that He still liked me. So I started singing a new chorus Sylvia's dad had taught us, which goes like this:

"It's a grand thing to be a Christian,
  It's a grand thing, I know."

And, that's all the important things that happened until we went up to Old Man Paddler's cabin, which I'm going to tell you about right now.

10

ONE COLD DAY our gang went up to see Old Man Paddler, although it wasn't very cold when we first started.

Nobody around our neighborhood had seen the old man for awhile because the weather had been very cold and snowy, so we supposed he had decided to stay in and keep warm. We knew he had plenty of wood to burn because, as I told you, there was a great big high rick right in the main room of his cabin, and there was another little room which was almost full of wood.

But even an old man had to eat, so our gang, with our parents saying we could, decided to take Poetry's big toboggan sled full of groceries and go up to the old log cabin in the hills where the old man lived to pay him a visit. A toboggan sled, you know, is one which generally doesn't have any runners at all but is made of long, flat, thin boards curved up at the front end.

Dad went to town in the morning of that day, which was Saturday, and got the old man's mail, about a half dozen letters (one from California) and two new magazines which the old man subscribed to, real Christian magazines like the ones most of our parents took. So we took the letters and magazines with us, knowing they'd help to make us welcome.

The sky was very clear and was as blue as one of my mom's summer morning glories when we started. Each one of us wore snowshoes, which look something like tennis rackets. Snowshoes have a long wooden frame with a network of sinews that look like Sylvia's snood stretched across it very tight. There are straps on each one, through which you push the toes of your shoes so the snowshoes won't come off while you're walking. When you have snowshoes on, if you know how to use them, you don't have to go around snowdrifts if you don't want to but can walk right on top of them and not sink in.

Pretty soon we had Poetry's toboggan packed and were ready to go. Each one of our mothers had given us something to take such as bread and butter, tin cans of milk, corn, and beans, and bacon and flour. Little Jim's mother sent some sassafras roots for making sassafras tea which was Old Man Paddler's favorite drink, and Little Jim's too ever since he'd learned how good it was.

It was about one o'clock in the afternoon when we started. We decided to follow the old wagon trail which winds around among the hills, getting higher and higher all the time. Years ago, our folks had told us, before the old man had taken his trip around the world and was gone so long everybody thought he was dead, the old wagon road had been pretty good, and the old man had owned a horse and wagon which he drove to town and back. The road was still there but it wasn't used anymore, and in some places fallen trees lay across it. And there were a lot of deep snowdrifts in it that day. We decided to follow it anyway so we'd be sure not to get lost, although Poetry had a compass on one end of his waterproof matchbox.

The compass looked kinda like a watch, only instead of having numbers on its face like watches do, it had letters: N for North; S for South; E for East; and W for West. A lot of letters which told you exactly which direction was which were in between. Instead of having two hands like watches do, the compass had just one, and it always pointed straight north, so you could always know which direction you were going.

On the other end of Poetry's waterproof matchbox was a magnifying glass called a burning glass, which first-class boy scouts know how to use to start a fire even when they don't have any matches. Poetry always carried his matchbox with him whenever we went on important trips, so we'd have a compass and not get lost. And we were always needing matches.

The only thing wrong with a winter day when the sun shines down on you and the snow looks like a great big white blanket spread all over the ground, and in some places the wind has made the snowdrifts look like big waves of white water, you keep wishing it wasn't so cold so you could go in swimming.

Big Jim and Circus walked on ahead, pulling the toboggan, doing what is called, "breaking trail," which means finding the best places to walk and walking there themselves so it would be easier for Little Jim and the rest of us to follow.

Dragonfly was just learning how to use snowshoes. Sometimes he would forget to lift the forward end of his foot before trying to take the next step, which is about the same as trying to step up on the curb when you're in town without lifting your foot first. If you don't lift your foot first, *kersquash* you go, headfirst in a snowdrift, which Dragonfly did maybe a dozen times until he learned to remember to lift his foot first. The first time he fell in we had to help him out because the drift was so deep. Sometimes you can't get out at all without kicking your snowshoes off first. We laughed at Dragonfly, and Poetry teased him by saying:

"Humpty Dumpty sat on a wall,
Humpty Dumpty had a great fall;

All the king's horses and all the king's men
Couldn't put Humpty Dumpty together again."

Then just about a minute later, Poetry forgot to lift his foot first and swaddle-de-dump-ker-sizzle, down he went headfirst in a great big, very soft snowdrift, and there he was complete-ly buried with his snowshoes kicking. And he couldn't get up or out until we helped him.

Big Jim stopped and came back to where we were. With all of us helping, we dragged Poetry back by the legs to a place where the snow wasn't so deep, only Dragonfly said it was kinda like dragging a hippopotamus. Then before Poetry could get up, Dragonfly who was still disgusted with him for calling him Humpty Dumpty, point-ed at him and yelled, "Look, Gang! This is the cow with the crumpled horn, that tossed the dog, that worried the cat, that caught the rat, that ate the malt that lay—"

Poetry rolled over quick and grabbed Dragon-fly by the leg, and down Dragonfly went again. Well, a wrestling match in a snowdrift, with snowshoes on, is fun to watch, so we watched until Big Jim stopped it and said we'd better go on.

It was a lot farther following the old wagon trail than the shortcut through the swamp which we took in the summertime. But of course it was safer, and it's silly for a boy to run any foolish risks just because he isn't afraid to. Dad says that being brave isn't half as important as having good sense.

It was half past two by Big Jim's watch when we came to the spring where the old man gets his water, which was about half a city block's distance from the cabin.

"Look!" Dragonfly cried. "There aren't any footprints or any path coming down to the spring." The snow was very deep there too. It had snowed hard last night, I thought, so maybe the old man hadn't shoveled a path yet because maybe he had enough water in the house to last him for the day.

"Here we go!" Big Jim shouted back to us, "Let's shovel a big wide path for him!"

Then Dragonfly yelled again, "There isn't any smoke coming out of the chimney!"

Without knowing why, I began to feel very queer inside. I remembered what the kind old man had said one day last summer when we'd told him we hoped he'd live forever. He had kinda laughed and said, "Live forever? That's exactly what I'm going to do, only I'm going to move out of this dilapidated old house first." And we knew he didn't mean his weathered old log house with its clapboard roof that looked like a picture of the house Abraham Lincoln was born in. He meant a wrinkled, white-haired old house with long white whiskers and gnarled old hands that trembled.

In a jiffy we were around where we could see the front door. Poetry, who had run on ahead, let out an excited gasp and squawked, "Look, everybody! The door's wide open and the floor's all covered with snow!"

Poetry was right. A big drift was right inside the door, and snow was all over.

For a minute not a one of us said a word. I thought, *What if he's already dead?* We stood and looked at each other kinda sadlike, like people do when they stand around in front of a church after a funeral, waiting for the pallbearers to come walking down the steps with the casket.

Then Big Jim said, "You boys wait a minute." My teeth were chattering for some reason, and it couldn't have been because I was cold because walking with snowshoes on will make you warm quicker than you can get warm standing around a fire, unless it's terribly cold. It was getting colder though. I think my teeth must have been chatting because I was afraid the old man was dead.

Little Jim had a very sad expression on his face.

We watched Big Jim go up to the open door. He took off one of his heavy mittens and gave four sharp raps with his knuckle and waited while I kept on holding my breath and feeling half scared and half excited. You know you ought never to walk into anybody else's house or even into his room without knocking first. Mom says it's a "law of etiquette" which has to be obeyed if you want to be polite.

Then Big Jim knocked again, and listened, and didn't hear anything. When he knocked the third time, and nobody answered, he called, "Hello! Anybody home?"

Still there was no answer. So he called back to us. "There's nobody here!"

We decided we'd better go in to see what was wrong, although there was already a sad picture in my mind of what we might see when we got in. I could imagine the old man lying there on the cot with his clean white whiskers covering his whole chest, and maybe his eyes would be shut and he would be dead. Or maybe he was already buried under the snow that had drifted in through the open door, there having been a very hard wind last night.

I kinda put my arm around Little Jim so he wouldn't shake so, and maybe so I wouldn't shake so much either.

"I'm not s-scared. I'm just c-cold," Little Jim said bravely. I guess that was the first time I'd noticed how much colder it was up here in the hills than it had been at home. It seemed almost twice as cold, although the sun was still shining and that helped some. There weren't any clouds in the sky except maybe two or three big white

96

ones that looked like a lot of big balls of cotton all piled together.

Big Jim stepped out of his snowshoes and stood them up just inside the cabin door, scooped about eight inches of snow off the step, and started to go in. Then he stopped dead still and straightened up with a jerk and listened.

I guess we'd all heard it at once, whatever it was. It sounded like the wind moaning in the trees, which it might have been, because the wind was beginning to blow a little. We all kept on listening, and we didn't hear anything else so pretty soon we were all inside the big room where the fireplace was, but Old Man Paddler wasn't there and there wasn't any fire. The cot over in the corner where he slept was empty. Poetry and Dragonfly hurried into the other room of the cabin to see if he was there, and he wasn't. That other room was kinda like our woodshed at home where Dad gives me all my lickings, which is as good a place as any because nobody can hear there except Dad and me, and the sounds that come out of our woodshed are not very musical.

Along the walls of that other room were high ricks of wood, heavy logs for the fireplace, and short, split wood for the cookstove. Pretty soon we were all back in the other room, standing beside the big snowdrift which we'd been walking on and which was kinda mashed down with our tracks. We kept looking at each other and feeling foolish because we thought we had heard somebody calling and yet there wasn't anybody there.

"I'm sure I heard somebody," Poetry said, and Dragonfly said the same thing, and so did I.

"I guess it was the wind in the trees outside," Big Jim decided, and as soon as we could, most of us decided the same thing.

"Where do you suppose he w-went?" Little Jim wanted to know.

Poetry, having a detective mind, began to look around for a note or something, and so did all of us.

Circus said, "Maybe he went to town to get his mail and hasn't come back yet."

"How'd the door get open?" Dragonfly wanted to know.

Poetry said, "The wind, of course."

All the time everybody was talking with nobody listening to anybody, like grown-up people do sometimes when there are a lot of them together. I kept thinking to myself, *I'm sure I heard a real voice!* Then all of a sudden I felt cold chills running all the way up my spine to my red hair, which tried to stand up under my cap but couldn't. I jumped like somebody had exploded a firecracker behind me, for as plain as day I heard it again, a kinda low moan. And it was right under the place where I was standing, which was all covered with snow.

11

YOU COULD HAVE KNOCKED us all over with a turkey feather! Big Jim whirled around as quick as a baseball player does when he tries to knock a homerun and misses the ball. Little Jim's face turned almost as white as the snow he was standing on. Circus looked up at one of the tie beams that goes across from one side of the cabin to the other as if he thought he'd heard something up there. Dragonfly's eyes were almost popping out of his head. Poetry was the only one of us who seemed to be thinking straight. He had a sort of detective mind. Then as quick as a hummingbird can flash from one flower to another, he was down on his knees, scooping the snow away from the floor. In a quick minute he had uncovered a steel ring that was fastened to the floor by a big staple, which is a horseshoe-shaped piece of metal with sharp points on each end, and the sharp points were driven into the floor.

We scraped away a lot more snow, and for the first time we noticed that somebody had cut a door in the floor, which meant that maybe there was a cellar down there. One end of the door was all covered with a big pile of wood. For the first time we noticed that some of the wood rick had tumbled over and fallen on the floor, only at first we'd thought it was just piled there on purpose.

But how'd a cellar get there? We'd been up to the cabin many times last summer, sometimes with Little Jim's bear, and there hadn't been any cellar then. But I remembered that day about six months before, just as we were leaving the old man to go up to the mulberry tree, he had stood up and said, "I must be getting on with my work now." He hadn't told us what his work was, and even though we had wanted to ask him, we hadn't because we thought maybe it wasn't any of our business.

All of a sudden Circus remembered something important, and he said, "Remember the big rug he always kept here?" And we remembered. That's why we'd never seen the door before.

Well, here it was as plain as day, a door cut in the board floor with one hinge showing and the other covered up with a big pile of wood. On the other side was a big steel ring, like that kind of doors always has, so you can lift the door up when you want to.

Then we heard the moan again, and we knew that somewhere down there was somebody who needed help. When a gang of boys knows some-body needs help, it doesn't take them long to start doing something. In less time almost than it takes to tell it, we had that pile of wood lifted up and leaning against a corner of the fire-place, and we were looking down into a great big hole under the cabin that looked as black as a barrel of tar. There was a stairway going down, but we couldn't see very well.

"Hello down there!" Big Jim called, while Little Jim's hand held on to mine so tight it almost hurt me.

Then somebody answered, and it was like a sad groan that said, "Hel—hello!" It was Old Man Paddler's quavery voice.

I knew then that he was still alive and I felt better. Little Jim sighed very loud, like some-body had given him a breath of fresh air. I looked at him quick, and his face looked kinda funny. I don't know what made me think of it, but I thought it looked like the face of one of the little lambs in my Bible storybook. Jesus was carrying the lamb in His arms, and it wasn't afraid.

Big Jim and Circus, being the oldest boys in our gang, went down into the cellar first, walk-ing down a narrow wooden stairway. Then Big Jim called for me to come too, which I did. It wasn't much of a cellar but it was a good place to keep things in the winter so they wouldn't freeze. Right away I saw Old Man Paddler, on the dirt floor, kinda half lying down and half sitting up. He was shivering with the cold. And one of his feet was twisted and swollen like it had been sprained or broken.

In my mind it was as plain as day what had happened. The dear old man had come down there to get something he was keeping there so it wouldn't freeze. Then he slipped on the stairs and fell and broke or sprained his ankle and couldn't get back up right away. Then maybe the wind had blown hard and burst open the outer door of the cabin which might not have been shut very tight, and it had bumped against the cellar door which was leaning up against the corner of the fireplace. There'd been a terribly hard wind last night, and maybe that had jarred the high rick of wood along the wall, and it had fallen down on top of the door. So the old man couldn't get out at all. Later we found out that was exactly what had happened.

Well, we had to act quick because Old Man Paddler was suffering, and he was so cold. *He's probably been here all night and all day today,* I thought. He tried to talk but his voice was so hoarse we couldn't hear him very well. It sounded like, "Get a fire started and get me in bed quick."

We knew he was right. It looked like he had a bad cold, and even an ordinary cold is dangerous if you don't take care of yourself. Doctors say

that even boys ought to go to bed when they
have a bad cold because if they do, they can get
well twice as quick. And when the doctor says to
go to bed and you don't you might even get pneumonia.

Well, with the old man having such a bad cold
and maybe a fever, and his being very old, he
might get pneumonia too.

I tell you we went to work like a whole nest
full of ants. Big Jim told us what to do, and we
did it as quick as we could. The first thing we
did was to help the old man up the stairs, take
his shoes off, and get him all covered up in bed.
It's a good thing he had long whiskers, I thought,
'cause that'd help to keep his chest warm.

There were a lot of things that had to be done.
We had to start two fires, one in the fireplace and
the other in the cookstove. We had to get some
water from the spring because all the water in
the house was frozen and wouldn't melt quick
enough to get him a drink. He had to have one
right away because he was very thirsty, which is
one of the reasons why we thought he must have
a fever. We had to unload our toboggan and get
some canned beef and vegetable soup because a
sick man has to have food that is easy to digest.

Circus and Dragonfly went to the spring for
water. Little Jim kinda stood close to Old Man
Paddler's bed and tried to get his gnarled old
hands warm by holding them in his and rubbing

them under the covers. Poetry pulled the toboggan inside and started to unpack it. And all the time it seemed to be getting colder and colder.

Big Jim and I laid the fire in the fireplace like boy scouts do. We hurried as fast as we could because we had to have hot water for the old man's sprained ankle, and he was shivering with the cold. All the time, while I was doing exactly what Big Jim said, I kept thinking, *What if he gets pneumonia? What if we didn't get here soon enough?*

First Big Jim wrinkled up some dry paper, and on top of it he put some little twigs and split sticks about half as big as a pencil, which I cut for him with the knife I'd found along Sugar Creek. My fingers were so cold they were getting numb. I never saw weather get cold so fast in my life.

All around and on top of the little sticks we put some broken, middle-sized sticks. I always did like to watch Big Jim start a fire. First there would be a little baby fire which crackled and sizzled and the little yellow flames would shoot up like little hungry yellow tongues that were begging for more wood to eat. It always made me think of Mom feeding Charlotte Ann, who would sit in her bassinet or in a chair and wait for the next bite, like the little baby fire waiting for us to feed it another stick of wood.

Pretty soon Big Jim straightened up and looked

around and said to Old Man Paddler, "Where are the matches?" just as Circus and Dragonfly came in from the spring with a kettle of water. Their faces were as red as a red sunset, on account of the cold, and there was ice frozen on the outside of the kettle where it had splashed over—it was that cold. They had even had to chop a hole through the ice at the spring to get the water.

Then Big Jim sent Poetry, Dragonfly, and Circus out to shovel the snow away from the door and to make a path down to the spring so it'd be easy to get more water when we needed it.

I guess Old Man Paddler hadn't heard Big Jim's question about the matches, so we asked him again.

The old man kinda sat up in bed and nodded to a shelf above the table where there was a matchbox. I hurried to get the box, and Big Jim opened it and looked in.

"It's empty," he said, and I thought his voice sounded kinda hollow.

When the old man heard Big Jim say, "It's empty," he tried to raise himself up again, and he said, "There's another box on the end of the shelf, I think." Then he sank back against the pillow and groaned a little, and I knew we'd have to hurry to get the room warm, or he'd be very sick.

I looked on the shelf, and Big Jim looked, and Little Jim looked. And there wasn't any matchbox! *What if we can't get a fire started at all?* I thought. *We'll all freeze to death!* Then, after we'd all three looked everywhere the old man told us to and still couldn't find any matches, I happened to remember Poetry's waterproof matchbox, so I ran to the door and yelled, "Hey, Poetry! Come here. *Quick!*"

Poetry, who was shoveling snow very fast to keep warm, straightened up, and in a fourth of a jiffy he and Dragonfly and Circus came puffing in. "What's the matter?" Poetry asked, looking from one to the other and at the little wigwam of sticks and paper in the fireplace.

"Give me your waterproof matchbox quick!" Big Jim commanded.

"Sure!" Poetry said. He put one end of his right mitten between his teeth, pulled his hand out, and shoved it into his coat pocket for the matchbox, which had a place for matches in the middle. It had a compass on one end and burning glass on the other, so in case you ever ran out of matches, you could start a fire with the glass, that is, if the sun was shining, which it still was that very minute.

All of a sudden Poetry's face took on a scared expression. He bit off the other mitten and began to run his short, fat hands into every pocket he had—his four pants pockets, two in front and two behind, and all his coat pockets.

And there wasn't any matchbox there! "I—I can't find it!" Poetry puffed, and I knew he must have lost it a half mile down the hill when he had fallen in the snowdrift, where he and Dragonfly had had their wrestling match.

12

No MATCHES! No magnifying glass!

That meant there'd be no fire. And it was getting colder all the time. Just that minute I heard Old Man Paddler cough like his cold was already going down on his chest.

We ought to get a doctor, I thought, and I knew it'd take us an hour and a half in the snow to get to a telephone and that whoever came would have to come on snowshoes, and that'd take another hour and a half. It'd be dark before then and with the wind beginning to blow, the snow would move like white dust on a dirt road when an automobile whizzes past. Even with a light the doctor couldn't see the way.

Big Jim opened the door and looked out at the thermometer hanging there. Then he shut the door quick and said, "It's below zero already." That was a lot colder than it had been at home.

For a minute, which seemed like an hour, we all stood looking at each other, none of us saying anything. I looked over at Little Jim, feeling especially sorry for him because he was so little.

Maybe I looked at him because he was such a good Christian, and I thought that pretty soon maybe he'd say something about God and that'd make us feel better. When a boy is in trouble and doesn't have his parents with him, he isn't quite as brave as he is most of the time, and he wishes he was a better Christian—if he is one. And if he *isn't* he wishes he was because as Sylvia's father had said the very Sunday before, it's silly not to be a Christian. If you aren't, you won't know how to pray and, if you should happen to die, then you'd be lost forever.

Do you know Little Jim's face wasn't scared at all? It was still as quiet as the lamb which Jesus carried in His arms in the picture in my *Child's Story Bible.*

It was Dragonfly who surprised us by saying, "Why don't we get down on our knees and pray?"

Well, why don't we? I thought. Of course, when a boy is in danger it is not always good to stop and pray because if there was a mad bull chasing a boy, it'd be silly to *stop* and pray. But he could pray on the run—and I'll bet he would too.

Now that I think of it, I guess I'd been praying in my mind ever since I knew Old Man Paddler was down in the cellar needing our help. Well, we knew God wouldn't send any matches right down out of heaven but He might help us find a match if there was one. In a jiffy there we all were, down on our knees besides Old Man Paddler's bed, like we'd been that night in the big brown tent in our town—that was in my last story, though.

Dragonfly's prayer was awful short because he was just learning how to pray out loud. I knew just what he was thinking about when he said with a tearful voice, "And if I don't see my p-parents again, I hope they'll all get saved before they die." I looked up for a second when he said that and saw the sun shining through the frost-covered window on the top of his cap. It was so cold none of us had thought to take his cap off, like you are supposed to do when you pray. But I think God knew how cold it was, and He always looks on the heart anyway, Mom says.

That prayer meeting wasn't more than three minutes long, and yet it must have been long in another way because it was long enough to reach all the way to heaven and back again. For in a jiffy there was what looked like an answer, right in front of our eyes!

You see, just as we got up from our knees, Old Man Paddler whispered for me to bring his Bible and his glasses, which I did, while the other boys kept looking for that extra box of matches which was supposed to be there and wasn't.

Well, I got the old man's Bible, which was as worn on the inside as it was on the outside. It

110

was while I was helping the old man put his glasses on that the idea came to me. Say, that idea just swooped down on me like a big chicken hawk swoops down on a little chicken in our barnyard in the summertime! There was our answer to prayer as plain as day. I could hardly believe it at first, for fear it wasn't so. And maybe it wouldn't work anyway, but the lenses in that old man's glasses were as thick as a magnifying glass! In fact, that is what they were. They made everything look bigger so he could see to read.

I was so excited I didn't even wait to hear the Bible verse the old man was going to read. "Look, Big Jim!" I almost screamed. "Look! Here's a *magnifying* glass! I'll bet you can start a fire with *it!*"

Poetry looked at me like he thought I was crazy, but I knew I was right—I hoped. Because I'd sat right close to Old Man Paddler at the Thanksgiving dinner and I had noticed how thick the lenses were and because I'm going to be a doctor someday—or maybe an eye doctor, which is an optometrist—I'd noticed them especially. I'd even borrowed them after dinner that day, and read a little bit just to see how I looked with them on.

Well, it was our last chance, because if we didn't hurry the sun would go down over the hill or else go behind clouds and stay there. We knew there wouldn't be any use to go back to look for

111

Poetry's matchbox because it'd be like looking for a needle in a haystack.

In a little while Big Jim was busy trying to start a fire. He held one of the lenses over his hand first to see if it would burn and it did. Big Jim knew just how to get the light focused. Pretty soon there was a little round spot of light on his hand about the size of a little pearl, just like a magnifying glass makes, and Big Jim said, "Ouch!" and jerked his hand away. It had actually been so hot it had burned him!

First he whittled some very thin shavings from a very dry piece of wood. Then he took some thin tissue paper which was wrapped around a present Little Jim's mom had sent along with us on the toboggan.

We all stood around shivering and standing close to each other to keep warm.

Well, Big Jim laid his little pile of shavings and the tissue paper in the lid of an old salve box, and then we held the door open a little crack so he could get the direct sunlight. "As soon as I get a blaze," he said, "I'll carry it to the fireplace, and pretty soon we'll all be warm."

It was easy to say, but it was harder to do. In only a few seconds though, I saw a little curl of smoke rise from the piece of tissue paper. Dragonfly gasped and crowded in closer. I looked around quick at Old Man Paddler. His eyes were shut and his lips were moving, which meant maybe he was praying. I knew he was, in fact. I thought, *What if Bill Collins was Old Man Paddler laying there like that, and some boys were trying to save my life? I'd do what he was doing too.*

When I looked back again at Big Jim, there was a hole burned through the paper but there wasn't any blaze. And all the little shavings did was smoke a little and go out.

Poetry, who had a good mind, said, "I'll bet if we had some kerosene, it'd burn."

We looked around and found an old-fashioned kerosene lamp which the old man used for light on the mantelpiece above the fireplace.

All the time Old Man Paddler lay there breathing kinda hard and with his eyes shut, like he was very sick or else like he was so sleepy he had gone to sleep. It didn't take Big Jim long to get the glass lamp chimney off and the lamp open. He twisted a piece of paper into a little roll, pushed it down into the kerosene, and a minute later he had one of the lenses of the glasses focusing the sunlight on the tip end of the kerosene-soaked paper.

I kept on shivering and hoping and thinking about my parents. We could all see our breath coming out of our noses and mouths like gray smoke coming out of a house with six chimneys.

"It won't work," Big Jim said, shaking his head and laying the glasses down on the table.

113

Then he put on his mittens and flapped his arms around his sides and slapped his hands against his legs to make the blood circulate better so he could get warm. The kerosene-soaked paper was even worse than plain paper. All it did was smoke.

Big Jim stopped flapping his arms around, took a deep breath, and sighed as he let it out. His breath almost hid him for a minute, like tobacco smoke does a man who smokes.

There was a sudden sound from behind us, Old Man Paddler making a noise like he was waking up and wanted to say something. "If you had some dry, decayed wood," he whispered, with his husky voice mixed up with his whisper, "you could start a fire." Then the old man shut his eyes and shivered and acted like he was asleep again, which I think he was.

"He's right," Big Jim said, "but there isn't any in the house." And there wasn't.

"I saw some once in a hollow tree right by the old swimmin' hole," Dragonfly said.

"There ought to be a hollow tree around here somewhere," Circus said. "I'll go look for one."

"I'll go with you," I said, but Big Jim said no, that he'd go himself.

Little Jim wanted to go, but he wouldn't let him either. Big Jim took Old Man Paddler's hatchet, and he and Circus went out into the snow where it was even colder than it was inside, and they started looking for a hollow tree which might have in it some very dry decayed wood, which is called "punk."

Say, the snow had already begun to drift because of the wind and that meant that pretty soon, even if the sun was still shining, the drifting snow would be almost as bad as clouds, and we *had* to have *sunlight* or we couldn't start a fire! I got to thinking about Mom and Dad and Charlotte Ann and wishing I'd been a better boy. I wished that right that very minute my great big dad would come walking through the door with a box of matches and his big strong voice would say, "Hello everybody! We'll have a roaring fire in just about a minute!"

There wasn't any use to wish that, I knew, but I kept on wishing it anyhow.

It seemed like Circus and Big Jim never would come back. I kept looking out the little hole where I'd wiped the frost off the window with my bare hand. I had to keep doing it or it would frost over again. It was so cold and getting colder all the time. I couldn't see very much though, except the trees and the snow that looked like the baby-powder Mom uses on Charlotte Ann. It kept blowing like white dust, with the wind picking it up and whirling it from one snowdrift to another, kinda like a little whirlwind does in the summertime when it picks up the dust from the road and carries it out across the cornfield. The sun was still shining though and I knew that if we'd find some punk pretty soon it still wouldn't be too late. If only we *could* find some!

After Circus and Big Jim had been gone for five or six minutes, which seemed like an hour, I made Dragonfly and Little Jim lie down on a blanket I found in a corner of the room. Then I wrapped it around them and went to look out the window of the other room. I couldn't see anything of Circus or Big Jim, but I thought I saw a big hollow tree that looked like it might have some punk in it. Before I knew what I was going to do, I decided to go out and look, which I did. First I told Dragonfly and Little Jim to lie still, which they promised to do.

I tell you it was cold, and it was very hard walking with those clumsy snowshoes on. I struggled as hard as I could, afraid any minute I might forget to lift my foot and I'd go down in a big drift and not be able to get out. And that is exactly what happened. The next thing I knew I was down in a huge drift that was as deep as I was tall. I couldn't get out without kicking my snowshoes off, and I couldn't seem to get them off. Big Jim and Circus weren't anywhere in sight and they couldn't have heard me holler for help anyway on account of the wind. I thought maybe I might not ever get out. While I was wallowing in that drift like a black bear wallowing in the mud in a swamp or my dad's big black hogs in

116

our barnyard mud puddle, I made a promise to God, "If You'll let me live, and Old Man Paddler, and all the Sugar Creek Gang, I'll never in all my life take a drink of beer or whiskey or smoke a cigarette or any kind of tobacco with its old nicotine poison in it, and I'll be the best soldier in the gospel army a boy can be. I'll always be kind to my mother, even when she tells me to do something I don't want to do."

Then I called for help as loud as I could, but nobody heard me. The wind on my face felt like a lot of little pygmies were shooting me with icicle arrows as sharp as needles.

After what seemed like a terribly long time, I began to get sleepy and didn't even want to get up at all, which is how you feel when you're about to freeze to death. If you lie down and go to sleep and nobody finds you, maybe you will freeze. So be sure never to give up when you're out in a snowstorm and begin to feel sleepy, but keep on working and walking because that'll help get you warm.

But I didn't know that then, so I just let myself give up and I lay down like I was going to bed in a great big feather bed. Pretty soon I'd wake up in heaven maybe.

The next thing I knew, Big Jim and Circus had found me. They were making me get up and walk, which I did without wanting to, being even disgusted with them for making me.

"Come on!" Big Jim gasped, pulling me by one arm and Circus pulling me by the other. "We've found some punk and we'll have a fire in no time!"

13

PRETTY SOON we were in the house where there wasn't any wind. Old Man Paddler still had his eyes shut and he acted like he was asleep. As soon as Big Jim could, he focused the sunlight on that little reddish-brown piece of decayed wood which was as light as a piece of paper and could be crushed in your hand almost as easy as a soda cracker could.

The very second that little round spot of concentrated sunlight touched that dry wood, it began to smoke. Big Jim's hands trembled a little because he was so cold. He had to brace his hand against the door to keep it steady.

Right away there was more and more smoke. Then I saw a little red glow of fire about the size of a pinhead, which grew bigger as Big Jim blew his breath on it while he kept on holding the spot of light in the same place, kinda moving it around a little so the fire would spread. His face was very serious. "Get me a piece of paper!" he ordered through his teeth. Then he held a little roll of tissue paper against the red coal and blew his breath on it, and kept on blowing, making the red coal bigger and making more smoke.

I tell you I felt like shouting, for right there before our eyes, a little yellow tongue of flame shot up, and there was our fire!

It didn't take Big Jim long to carry that tiny paper torch over to the little wigwam of sticks and paper in the fireplace. From then on we were just like a bunch of noisy blackbirds, with all of us feeding the little fire-baby a little stick whenever Big Jim would let us. Soon there was a roaring fire that made us feel mighty good.

We started another fire in the cookstove, boiled some water, made sassafras tea and hot beef and vegetable soup for Old Man Paddler, and put hot, wet towels on his swollen ankle.

Say! You should have seen that old man get better and brighten up! As soon as it was warm in the cabin, he let us prop him up in bed. When the soup was ready, Poetry, who had seasoned it because he was the best cook of any of us, carried a great big steaming bowlful to the old man.

Before he ate, the old man's hoarse voice whispered, "I think we ought to be thankful, boys," and in a second he closed his eyes for prayer. He couldn't bow his head very well because he was leaning back against the pillows we had put there for him. He nearly always prayed with his face looking up anyway. It was awful quiet in the cabin while we waited for him to begin. I could hear the wind outside, whirring around the cabin, the fire roaring in the cook stove and crackling and sizzling in the fireplace.

I tell you that was a grand prayer. First he thanked God for answering *our* prayers. Then he thanked Him for the Sugar Creek Gang, calling us all by our nicknames like he always did. He finished by saying, "Bless Little Tom Till and Bob Till and all the boys in the world who don't have Christian parents to take them to Sunday school and church and teach them to love Jesus and live right. Help all the Christian pastors and school teachers and senators and congressmen and all the leaders of our country to do something about saving our boys. And help the leaders in other countries not to forget the millions of boys that are living all around them. Bless the parents especially."

For some reason, while the old man was praying, I began to like my mom and dad better than ever and to be very proud of them. I wished that right that very minute I could go running lickety-sizzle from the kitchen of our house into the living room and make a dive for my mom and dad and give them a great big hug, like I do sometimes when I happen to see them standing together somewhere hugging each other, like parents do. Then I wished I could scoop little Charlotte Ann up in my arms and hold her wobbly little head with its soft cheeks and pug nose

121

up against my freckled face and give her a hug too.

It was while Old Man Paddler was eating his soup that Little Jim remembered about the mail which was one of the reasons we had come up there in the first place.

Old Man Paddler took the letters one at a time in his wrinkled old hands, holding them up kinda close to his eyes and looking at them through his thick glasses. I didn't like it very well that he had to wear glasses because I liked to see his kind old eyes twinkle, and I couldn't because of the glasses. You see, he had so many whiskers you couldn't tell whether he was smiling unless you saw his eyes.

Well, with the cabin nice and warm and with Old Man Paddler feeling better and maybe not going to be very sick at all—except that he couldn't walk on his sprained ankle and would have to stay in bed for awhile till it got well and until his cold was better—and with all of us drinking sassafras tea, we forgot about how cold it was outside. We sat around the fireplace, just thinking and talking and feeling cheerful, when the old man surprised us by saying, "I suppose you boys remember my nephew, Barry Boyland, who was shot last summer?"

We'd nearly forgotten about him. In fact, I hadn't thought about him more than once, and that was when my city cousin, Walford, had asked about him the day I killed our old Thanksgiving turkey—Say! That, crazy, ignorant Airedale dog! He should have had more sense than to try to chase a cat while he was tied to a turkey's neck! But dogs are like that, even funnier than girls that think boys are afraid of spiders, which I'm not.

Then the old man said something that made us feel sad again. He said, "I've been thinking about the will I made in which I put something for each member of the Sugar Creek Gang."

Then he stopped talking and turned the letter from his nephew over in his hands. We just sat looking at him, and listening to the wind and the fire and waiting for him to talk on. Pretty soon he did. "It's the Till boys I'm thinking about," he said, "Tom and Bob, whose father is an infidel. I am very glad that Little Tom is going to Sunday school regularly, and I think it is fine the way you boys have been treating Bob even though he is your enemy. I think I ought to tell you that I'd like to have them in my will too, and they can be if—" Then the old man stopped talking for a minute.

I felt an exclamation point rising up out of my head like they do in cartoons in the newspaper when people are astonished about something. For a minute I didn't like the idea because I didn't like Bob Till. I liked little mean-faced, red-haired Tom though. But Bob was so wicked and he said such awful words and hated Sunday school and was so ignorant he thought boys who loved Jesus were sissies.

None of us said anything for a minute. In fact, we didn't say anything at all, although I saw Poetry's eyes and he looked at me disgusted. Then I looked at Little Jim but he still looked like the little lamb I told you about.

The old man tore open his nephew's letter, which was from California, and started to read it. But he didn't because there was something else he wanted to say first. Then he explained to us what his will said, and that was that anybody that was a member of the Sugar Creek Gang could get in on the will, and it was up to us who we got to join the gang, but that nobody could join unless he wanted to. "Don't worry about there not being enough for everybody," he said, "because there is."

Then the old man told us one of the most important things in the world. I can't explain it very well even if I do understand it myself. But anybody that wants to have everlasting life and have all his sins forgiven forever and go to heaven can have it all for nothing if he'll repent of his sins and let Jesus save him. It's all in God's WILL which Jesus made when he died. There's enough everlasting life and forgiveness for everybody, and there's plenty of room in heaven because God owns the whole world and all of heaven and a million stars and planets. And the only thing that'll keep people from getting into God's will is their sins which they won't be sorry for and won't quit doing and their unwillingness to open the door of their stubborn hearts to let Jesus in.

Well, I certainly liked to hear the kind old man explain things about the Bible, but I knew it was hard for him to talk on account of his cold. Even while he was explaining it, though, I was making up my mind to try to get Tom Till into both wills.

I guess I was thinking about that letter from Barry Boyland which was lying on the pretty, many-colored Indian blanket on the old man's bed. That is, it had been, for just that minute the old man raised his knees and the letter fell off on the little brown rug beside the bed.

Circus made a dive for the letter and handed it back to the happy old man who lifted it close to his eyes and began to read it. We could tell the letter had something very interesting in it because even though we couldn't see his eyes very well, we could tell by the way his whiskers moved that the letter was making him happy and that there was a smile buried away down there somewhere.

When we found out what the letter said, there were six of the broadest smiles on six of the happiest boys you ever saw. What do you suppose that letter said?

"Will you read it out loud?" the old man asked

Big Jim, maybe because he was our leader. The old man took off his glasses, and about twenty twinkles were in his eyes.

This is what Big Jim read, and what we listened to:

Dear Uncle Seneth [That's Old Man Paddler's first name],

Thank you very much for the check for $1,000 which came yesterday. I think your plan to give the Sugar Creek Gang a vacation next year is a very good one.

This morning I drove up to San Francisco and spent nearly half a day looking at new house trailers, and I believe I have exactly what we want. The trailer is twenty feet long, is very beautiful and thoroughly modern, with two folding beds, a bed, a gas stove for cooking, a clothes closet, an icebox and everything needed for a real camping trip. I expect to live in it this winter like you told me to, so I'll know all about how to use it.

I think you ought to tell the Sugar Creek Gang about it right away so they can make their plans ahead of time and have something to look forward to. Tell them that I'll be driving past Sugar Creek along about July 5 or 6 next year and to be ready. I haven't decided yet where we'll camp but I think it'll be near a lake somewhere. Tell Poetry to have his tent ready because some of the boys will have to sleep in it. They may take turns if they like. Bill will need his binoculars, and each boy will need his New Testament as well as fishing rod and swimming suit. A warm sweater will come in handy too in case we go up into the north woods where it gets cold at night, even in July.

Perhaps Big Jim ought to bring his rifle because if we do go up north, there'll be wildcats in the woods that might get a little too friendly. . . .

There was more in the letter but that was all that especially concerned us. Boy oh boy! That was enough too! Talk about a flock of noisy blackbirds! We were even worse!

Think of it! A trailer camping trip in the north woods! For two whole weeks next summer! Of course we'd have to get our parents' permission, but that'd be easy 'cause our parents knew what was good for boys.

Now, I am very sorry to say that I'll have to end this story right here, 'cause it's long enough. I can't even tell you about how we had to stay all night in the cabin because of a terrible blizzard that came up before we could start home, but everything came out all right, even if our parents did worry about us, and nearly a dozen men came up in the middle of the night to find out if we were all right.

Even if this story wasn't long enough, I couldn't tell you about our camping trip because it hasn't happened yet. But just as soon as summer comes and it's all over, I'll sit right down the very first thing and write about it for you. I think I'll even name the next story "The Sugar Creek Gang Goes Camping."